I0720395

His Majesty's Hounds— Book 3

Sweet and Clean Regency Romance

Giving a Heart of Lace

Arietta Richmond

Dreamstone Publishing © 2017

www.dreamstonepublishing.com

ISBN: 1925499499

ISBN-13: 978-1-925499-49-0

Disclaimer

This story is a work of fiction.

Names, characters, places and incidents are the product of the author's imagination and are used fictitiously. Any resemblance to events, locales or actual persons, living or dead, is entirely coincidental.

Books by Arietta Richmond

His Majesty's Hounds

Claiming the Heart of a Duke

Intriguing the Viscount

Giving a Heart of Lace (a prequel to Winning the Merchant Earl)

Being Lady Harriet's Hero

Enchanting the Duke (coming soon)

Redeeming the Marquess (coming soon)

Healing Lord Barton (coming soon)

Winning the Merchant Earl (coming soon)

Loving the Bitter Baron (coming soon)

Rescuing the Countess (coming soon)

Attracting the Spymaster (coming soon)

The Derbyshire Set

A Gift of Love (Prequel short story)

A Devil's Bargain (Prequel short story - coming soon)

The Earl's Unexpected Bride

The Captain's Compromised Heiress

The Viscount's Unsuitable Affair

The Count's Impetuous Seduction

The Rake's Unlikely Redemption

The Marquess' Scandalous Mistress

A Remembered Face (Bonus short story – coming soon)

The Marchioness' Second Chance (coming soon)

A Viscount's Reluctant Passion (coming soon)

Lady Theodora's Christmas Wish

The Duke's Improper Love (coming soon)

Other Books

The Scottish Governess (coming soon)

The Earl's Reluctant Fiancée (coming soon)

The Crew of the Seadragon's Soul Series, (coming soon - a set of 10 linked novels)

Dedication

For everyone who had the grace to be patient while this book, and the ones before and after it, were coming into existence, who provided cups of tea, and food, when the writing would not let me go, and endured countless times being asked for opinions.

For the other writers in my Regency Romance mastermind group, who inspire me, and ask the kind of questions that make us all learn more about this fascinating period.

For the readers coming to know these characters well, and who inspire me to continue, by buying my books!

For my growing team of beta readers and advance reviewers – it's thanks to you that others can enjoy these books in the best presentation possible!

And for all the writers of Regency Historical Romance, whose books I read, who inspired me to write in this fascinating period.

Chapter One

The coal box was empty. The larder contained some cheese, some bread, and very little else. Serafine walked to her room with a heavy heart. In her dresser drawer there was a small metal chest – the sort that, in another life, she might have used as a jewellery box.

She turned the key, and opened the chest. She stared at the contents, as despair gripped her. The box contained only ten pounds. Ten pounds that were their last remaining money. And, carefully wrapped in a scrap of silk, a heart made of lace and ribbon and beads, all sewn onto a piece of parchment.

Lace that was all she had left of her grandmother. Everything else had been sold. Sewing that heart had been just for fun, then – it seemed an eternity ago – before *'the fall'* as she thought of it. Before her fool of a brother had gambled away everything, drawn into a tawdry gaming hell by that demon Pendholm, and bled of everything that had any value in their lives. Before her brother had committed the ultimate betrayal, and killed himself because of it.

Before the *ton* had shunned them for the scandal of a suicide in the family. Before…..

She shut the thoughts away. At least they had the house. It was small, and in a rather unfashionable part of town – not quite respectable at all – but it was her mother's outright, left to her by her aunt, shortly after Serafine's father's death. Although an unheated house, with no servants, and little furniture left was not exactly the most pleasant place to live, at least it was theirs.

She took out two pounds, her finger absently stroking the lace as she did, then shut and locked the chest, hiding it away again. Today, she could buy food and coal. What would she do on the day when there was no longer any money to do so?

~~~~~

Serafine sighed, holding the bag of food close against her. It was heavy, but she treasured the weight – it was the substance of survival, at least for a little longer. The coal would be delivered later in the day – enough for a month, if she was very careful. The food would not last near so long.

Passing the shop on the corner, she paused to look in the window a moment. Once, she would have thought such a shop beneath her – now, what it contained was as far beyond what she could afford as the moon was above the earth. Yet she still liked to look at pretty things. A little collection in one corner of the window caught her eye. A pile of what might be called favours – little cards and items, decorated with ribbons, lace and sometimes paste gems or feathers.
~~~~~

Pretty little nothings that a man might give his mistress, or a woman he was courting.

One, in particular, a little sta ned on the edges, but still pretty, reminded her of the heart with her grandmother's lace – it was the sort of thing that some called a Valentine. She stared at it for a while, feeling as if it was important, but not knowing why, then shrugged, lifted her bags again, and went home.

~~~~~

The next day was clear and brignt, but very cold – they would likely have snow on Christmas Day. Serafine sat at the window of the parlour, sewing. She was nearly finished embellishing the gown for Mrs Johnson, which was a relief, for it meant that she would be paid for the work, but also a worry, for there were no more dresses waiting her attention. And her sewing was their only income –the only way to stretch out what money they had, for a little longer.

The ladies of the merchant classes, who lived all around them, those who had some money, but were not rich enough to ever consider going to a modiste in the heart of London, they were her customers. They found the idea of a Lady born sewing for them somehow satisfying (not that anybody ever called her 'Lady Serafine' any more – that manner of address belonged to *before* – now she was just 'miss' most of the time. And to those who knew her name at all, she was Miss Sera – Serafine had seemed a lovely name to her mother, who was fascinated by old mythology and similar, but now it was simply out of place for her current station in life.).
~~~~~

The merchant ladies appreciated her fine sense of fashion. But more than that, they appreciated her affordable pricing.

She hummed as she worked, her clever fingers sewing beads onto a tracery of lace on the hemline of the dress, but her mind was elsewhere.

Her thoughts kept going back to that sad little pile of favours in the shop window. She wondered if they sold well, and what sort of people bought them. She'd seen a few things like that... *before*... but she'd never thought much of it. She thought of it now. They were such little things, and sewing them was, she suspected, not so different from sewing embellishments onto dresses.

Were they a thing that members of the *ton* might buy? Perhaps – if someone important bought one, or gave one to someone noticeable... if that happened, then others would follow – there were always those who simply copied everything the arbiters of fashion did, or the royal family did. She brought her attention back to sewing the last few beads onto the dress – what a goose she was, dreaming about the royals and the *ton*! They had nothing to do with her world now, nothing at all.

Chapter Two

Mr Raphael Morton was bored. That was a terrible thing to admit, when what he was doing was going over the business ledgers with the man he employed to do his accounts. Mr Manning was excellent at his job, and the ledgers were neat and clear. They showed just how wealthy Raphael was – just how well Morton Empire Imports was doing. Most men would be excited by what they saw – not bored.

But, bored he was. For Raphael, the exciting part was the planning, laying out the path that led to this, that ensured that, if all the steps were followed, the wealth would grow. After years at war, the inactivity of sitting in an office, or walking the warehouse and speaking to customers, was slowly driving him mad. To make it worse, his ship's captains came back not only with cargoes of exotic goods to make him even wealthier, but with tales of distant lands, strange sights and different people.

He envied them. He wanted to see those places himself. No amount of wealth and rich living here could change that. London was a gilded cage.

For, no matter what they had vowed to each other, the world would go as it did – his friends, those who had been closer than family for those long years of war, would be forced away from him. It was simple fact. They were all titled, and he was not. He was, in fact, that worst of things (from the *ton's* point of view), a Cit – a merchant, one tainted by dirtying his hands with trade. No matter that it had made him wealthier than most of them, no matter that they craved the luxuries he imported, he was, to the *ton*, to be disdained for his lower class existence.

How could his friends ever overcome that? He would not wish them shunned by their peers for associating with him. Yet he missed them sorely. Better to travel the world alone, than to live here in luxury, so close, yet never able to see them.

"That will do for today, Manning. Your work is excellent, as usual. Make sure that the Captain of the Morton Venture receives a suitable bonus – he has done far better than I expected with this cargo."

Manning blinked in some surprise, for they were barely half way through the review of the ledgers, then nodded, closed the books, and left the office.

~~~~~

Two hours later, Raphael was still sitting there, thinking. He had reached the rather depressing conclusion that there was no easy answer to his boredom, or to his sense of being trapped. Perhaps it might be more bearable if he had something new and different to do, some new venture?
~~~~~

At least then he could sink himself into the planning, into bringing something new to life, and making it profitable. But what? He had warehouses full of exotic materials, objects, spices and other things – was there some new way that he could use them, something new he could create, that could be cleverly brought to the attention of the most influential of the *ton*, or perhaps even the Prince Regent? Raphael knew that, for something new to become a profitable venture, it would have to draw the attention of those with money to spend.

The idea took hold, it was a puzzle to be solved – what new thing could he create, using goods that he already had, which could take the fashionable people by storm, and make him even wealthier? (not that he cared about the money, he had enough – it was the challenge that mattered...)

He spent the next few days stalking through his warehouses, looking at everything, terrifying his managers and warehouse labourers, who were certain that he must be seeking evidence of wrongdoing on their part. He could feel an idea, an insight, at the edge of his thoughts – but it refused to surface. He went home to toss and turn in restless sleep, dreaming of exotic oddities.

~~~~~

With Mrs Johnson's dress completed and delivered, Serafine took a little of the money that she had been paid, and went to the market. She would add some more food to their supplies while she could, and getting out and walking felt good, after the last few days of sitting and sewing.
~~~~~

At the little shop on the corner she stopped, looking at the items in the window again. Surprised at what she saw, she considered a moment, then turned and entered the shop.

"What can I do for you, Miss?"

The shopkeeper looked at her, obviously assessing her possible wealth from her clothes.

"In the window – those little… favours? I noticed them the other day, and meant to come in earlier – I particularly liked the heart shaped one, but I can't see it now – has it been sold?"

"Oh yes Miss, you've got to be quick to get a nice one of those – they sell all the time, any that I get. The young gents are always looking for tokens to give the girls they're courting. The heart shaped ones go fastest – seems they like it to be obvious what they mean when they put it in the girl's hands. Don't often get a young lady asking about them though."

Serafine thought for a moment, as the shopkeeper waited, his expression curious.

"Where do they come from? I mean, who do you buy them from?"

"Well Miss, it's not always the same. Used to be my old mother made some for me, but she's gone to God now, and m'wife don't like to sew fiddly things. So now it's only when someone brings some in, that they want to sell, that I can get any. Pity, because there's always those as wants to buy 'em."

"How much do you sell them for?"

Serafine waited for the answer, almost holding her breath.

When the shopkeeper, after some time thinking, named a figure, she was pleasantly surprised, even though she suspected he might have inflated the number, because he thought she looked like she could afford more. That idea almost brought a bubble of bitter laughter to her, but she repressed it. An idea was forming — maybe there was a way for her to earn more, to keep them surviving a bit longer.

"What if I had some to sell you? New ones, heart shaped ones with pretty beads or ribbons, not just lace?"

The shopkeeper's eyes narrowed with avarice, and Serafine knew, instantly, that her instinct was right — this *was* a way to earn more.

"Likely I'd be interested in buying... if the price was right..."

Twenty minutes of haggling later, Serafine left the shop, with a bounce in her step that hadn't been there for a long time. They had agreed that she would bring him three as a sample, in a few days' time. For those, he would give her about half of the price he normally sold them for. If they sold well, he would buy more — and give her a better percentage of the price, especially if she made things that he could sell for a higher price to begin with.

By her calculations, she could earn as much from making four or five of the pretty little favours as she could from embellishing a dress — and she would need to use less materials to do so. After a quiet luncheon with her mother, who declared it far too cold to go out, and wanted only to huddle by the fire and read, Serafine went out again — to buy beads and lace, and some heavy paper.

It was time to get to work.

~~~~~

Some hours later, tired but satisfied, she carefully put away the collection of beads, laces and little paste gems that she had bought – the amount it had cost her, even buying mismatched and second-hand (for small favours did not need many beads, unlike dresses!), worried her, for it had taken far more of their money than she was comfortable with, but there really was no choice – she had to earn money somehow, and that meant spending some first.

If these did well, though, she would need to find another source of materials – both to get better quality, and because, with today's purchases, she had quite exhausted the supply from the places she usually shopped.
~~~~~

Chapter Three

Christmas Day arrived with a deep fall of snow overnight, after which the day dawned clear and beautiful, the winter sun making the icicles on the trees and eaves sparkle like decorations. For Seraphine and her mother, it was a day of sadness – their second Christmas since *'the fall'* - and now they were considerably poorer than they had been for the first one. They missed James, her brother – for no matter how much Serafine might curse what he had done, he was still her brother – and his absence hurt.

There was enough coal to warm one room of the house – it had to be enough. And, taking Serafine completely by surprise, Mrs Johnson, and two of the other ladies whose dresses she sewed, had sent their servants to her door bearing a hamper of Christmas food and a bottle of good wine. The simple kindness had brought her to tears.

Between that, and the success of her first few favours, the money would last a little longer, and that was, at least, something to be grateful for.

Curled by the fire, Serafine was thinking about favours. The first few that she had made were Christmassy – in the hope that young men might buy them to give to their sweethearts for the Holiday. She had tried, as much as possible with the cheap materials, to make them look expensive, to make them look like the sort of thing that a member of the *ton* would not be ashamed to give.

It seemed that she had succeeded, for Mr Tanner at the shop had been impressed, and she was sure that he had sold them for even more than he had originally thought he might. She had seen his eyes narrow with avarice again, when she unwrapped them from the box she had brought them in. She might have pushed for more than he had paid her, but she was grateful for what she received – and anyway, if she wanted him to buy more, it was best not to make that too hard for him.

She had gone back two days later to see if any of them had sold, and been startled to discover that they all had – and that he would like more, as soon as she could make them. So she had. And now she had used up almost all of the materials she had bought. The money from those favours would, with care, keep them in coal until the weather got a little warmer. But she would need to make more – Mrs Johnson and her friends only had so many dresses in need of work, and there was nothing else to provide an income.

So she stared into the flames and worried. She worried about what sort of favours she should make next – what holidays or events might there be, that would encourage people to buy favours for their mistresses or for the girls that they courted?

And even more, she worried about where she would get some more suitable materials, without having to use money that they would need for food. Whatever else happened, she would not see her mother starve, after all that they had been through. She dreamed of the sort of shop that she used to buy her ribbons and gloves and bonnets from, before, when she was a Lady, when she had money and no idea of what it was to be poor, or reviled. Oh to have even a tiny bit of the sort of ribbons and lace that could be bought in such a shop!

As her eyes drifted shut in the quiet room, a tiny thought floated through her mind, just before sleep took her:- *'where did those shops get their stock from?'*

~~~~~

For Raphael, Christmas was also strange – there was the joy of actually being there to celebrate it with his mother, sister, and brother, yet the sadness of his father's empty chair. He missed his father with an intensity that had caught him off guard – and he deeply regretted that war had taken him away, when the business had grown so astoundingly in his father's talented care. There was so much that he might have learnt, had he been at his father's side.

There was also the truly odd feeling of not even knowing exactly where the other Hounds were. After more than four years together at war, their tight knit band of specialists, called 'His Majesty's Hounds' by most of the rest of their troops, for their uncanny ability to find and deal with French spies, and to predict French troop movements, they had become almost more family than his family.
~~~~~

Christmas without them seemed somehow wrong, somehow a betrayal of the bond between them.

He felt cast adrift, trying to be a serious merchant, running what had become a vast empire of trade, yet totally unsure of his own place in the world, now that he had to deal with the rules of society. Over the last few weeks, since the day when he had realised just how bored he was, he had repeatedly thought about his wish to travel – and the complete impossibility of doing so. And the puzzle that he had set himself that day, of finding something new to sell, some new way to leverage what he had, still nagged at him. He had no answer. He would find one yet.

"Raphael's not listening, Mother. I don't think he heard any of what I just said!" Isabella's voice was somewhere between teasing and petulant, for, after so long of not having Raphael there, she could not truly be angry with him.

Raphael realised, with a start, that he had, indeed been wool-gathering – had been drifting off into his puzzle, oblivious to the conversation around him.

"I wasn't completely ignoring you, Bella. I do know that you were talking about dresses and Balls, and eligible young men, and bemoaning the fact that we are not of the aristocracy, so that you will not be invited to any of the truly fashionable events." The fact that he could not remember anything of exactly what she had said did not prevent his summary from being accurate. She turned her huge dark eyes upon him and proceeded to look like a hurt puppy.

"Well, it isn't fair! We can afford dresses and jewellery just as beautiful as theirs – why should not being titled matter?"

His sister had an alarmingly revolutionary attitude to some things, he thought with chagrin. Whilst he could rather sympathise with her sentiment, that attitude could make her life somewhat difficult, given the oh so rigid rules of society.

Gabriel was uninterested in his sister's complaints – at 16, he was just growing into himself, with the shape of the handsome man just beginning to emerge from the boy. He was, however, most interested in doing justice to the remarkable Christmas Feast that their chef had produced. Raphael watched him with affection, and prayed that Gabriel need never go to war, need never see any of the things that he had seen, need never know the terrible things that men could do to each other. He hoped that Gabriel would join him in running the business – but that was at least two years off, for he would have the best education possible before then.

Isabella was speaking again, and he had missed part of the conversation... again.

"...quite beautiful – so intricately worked – a little heart, with ribbon and lace and little bells and holly berries on it. It must mean that he truly cares for me, mustn't it, mother?"

What on earth was she talking about? Raphael wondered, as the conversation continued.

"Now my dear, perhaps he does have a *tendre* for you... or perhaps he simply wishes to outdo your other admirers..." Their mother's voice was filled with affection and amusement and she watched her daughter consider that comment.

"No, no, he must really care. You don't understand – I will have to show you!"

Completely ignoring any sort of ladylike behaviour, Isabella rose and ran from the room, to return a few minutes later, with something cradled in her hands.

"You see?" She deposited it on the table for them to examine.

Raphael, curious, scooped it up. It was a piece of heavy, parchment like paper, folded in two so that a message could be written inside, and decorated on the outside with lace, ribbon and gems (which were almost certainly paste), with tiny paste holly berries in a cluster, and two even smaller dangling bells. The whole thing was cut to a heart shape. It was, he had to agree, charming. He had seen things like this before, on the occasion of Saint Valentine's Day, and at other times attached to bouquets and gifts. This was both more elaborate and, strangely, more elegant than any he had seen before.

Just as he went to open it, and see just what message had been written for Bella, she snatched it from his grasp.

"Oh no – that message is for me, it's private. You can't read it!"

"As you wish." Raphael made great show of turning away and becoming uninterested, which only made Isabella make a little huff of expelled breath in exasperation. Tilting her nose up, she turned away.

"I think I shall remove myself to the parlour." He watched her leave the room with a fond smile But the image of that exquisitely wrought little piece of frivolity stuck in his mind. Why did it seem significant?

Chapter Four

Within a few days, the pristine white snow of Christmas morning had turned to half melted muddy piles of icy slush on London's busy streets. People ventured on their way with care, in boots or with pattens on their feet if they could afford it. Serafine set out that morning in her best remaining winter dress, with the pelisse that was still mostly respectable over it. She had woken from her nap on Christmas Day with the memory of that passing thought. And now she felt compelled to investigate – *where did the shops that sold pretty trifles to the nobility buy their goods?*

She went back towards the more fashionable parts of the city, back towards her past... She sought out the shops that were close to, but not on, the most fashionable streets. Shops that would have been beneath her... before... And therefore, shops where she would not be recognised. She could not bear to face the cut direct from those she had once called friends – she would not allow herself to risk that again.

At least she must have managed to look like a Lady should, for a scruffy crossing sweeper leapt out to sweep the snow and detritus from her path as she crossed the street. She tossed him the smallest coin she had – she could ill afford to, yet she would not see anyone starve – not now that she knew the feel of true hunger herself. She received a few curious looks – a young gentlewoman out without a maid beside her - but she ignored them. Just ahead was exactly the sort of shop she was seeking.

Inside, the shop was small, yet full of many beautiful things. An older woman, well dressed, yet in garments some years out of fashion, was seated behind a small counter. She rose as Serafine entered.

"Good day to you, my Lady, what may I help you with today?"

Serafine almost laughed – it was so long since anyone had called her 'my Lady' that it almost sounded wrong. She looked around, and wandered through the shop, drawn from display to display, with so many beautiful items to explore.

"I am not sure – I would like to simply look for a little – to see what appeals to me most."

"Certainly, my Lady, do ask me if you wish to know about anything, or see anything else." The woman sat again, quietly waiting, and watched her every move.

In the back corner of the shop, jumbled in a little basket on a shelf, she found a collection of scraps of lace, short pieces of ribbon, broken pieces of paste jewellery, little feathers, and other interesting things. She took it to the counter.

The old woman looked at her in surprise, but waited for her to speak.

"This basket of things – how much? I know it may seem strange, but I like to make small things, for my friend's children's dolls, and other little things – all of these pieces are interesting, and I can use tiny amounts like this."

The woman smiled at her, seeming to find the explanation reasonable – for many ladies of the nobility amused themselves with charitable works and most embroidered or sewed small trifles. Waiting for the answer, Serafine ran her fingers through the tangle of items – some pieces were unusual – in colour or texture, or in the shape of small silver or carved stone beads.

"Where do these come from?" She hoped that her question sounded casual enough.

The woman looked at her again, and named a price for the little basket – a remarkably reasonable price, considering the location of the shop. As Serafine produced the money to pay, the woman went on, finally getting to the answer that Serafine really wanted.

"Where do they come from? Things come from all over the world, from India and beyond – China and the East Indies, from Africa, from many places – sometimes materials are brought here, and made into things here, sometimes they are imported complete. The merchant companies get very wealthy finding exotic trinkets to keep the *ton* happy. I buy things from only the better importers – I like to sell quality to the quality!" She gave a small laugh at her own words, and Serafine joined her.

~~~~~

"I've never thought about it before, but when I saw all of these things, and touched them, I couldn't help but wonder." She smiled at the woman, hoping that she might say more.

"You'd be a rare one to think about it. Most of the young Ladies I sell pretty things to don't care where they come from. There're some good merchants now. Now that the war's over, more goods can get here, shipping's safer, they tell me. The good ones even charge a bit less, now there's less risk in their business. For those who've got a taste for the exotic or the unusual, and good quality, I buy from Morton Empire Imports. That's a sad tale though. Old Mr Morton, God rest his soul, the poor man died before his son got home from war – such a sorry thing!"

It seemed that Serafine had unleashed a flood of words. Perhaps the woman rarely had anyone to talk to – anyone who had the slightest interest in her business or her life, that is.

"There's other companies, but Morton is the best of the bunch – never had a faulty shipment from them, not once!"

After letting the woman ramble on for another twenty minutes, Serafine finally extracted herself from the shop, her purchases in hand, and took herself home. Now she not only had some more materials to work with, but a name. What if she could buy materials direct from the importer? Surely that would be cheaper, or at least better quality for the same amount of money. She would have to find out where this Morton Empire Imports had its office.

~~~~~

A few days later, when Serafine delivered the next batch of favours to Mr Tanner's shop, he greeted her with great enthusiasm.

"Good day to you Miss, I do hope that you've got some more of your excellent work for me?"

That was more flattery than usual from him – she wondered why. She didn't have to wonder long – he could hardly contain himself.

"Those last few – the Christmas heart ones – I sold the smallest of them to young Jemmy – works as a groom at the Arbuthnot place – they're the second wealthiest merchants around, don't you know. You'll never guess what happened next! Mr Arbuthnot – Porter his name is, he's the son of the house – saw it, and he liked it so much he actually came here, to buy one for the girl he's sweet on. Now that's the sort of customer I like! He bought the biggest one – that nice one with the little bells - didn't even blink at the price."

Mr Tanner was so excited at the idea of such a wealthy customer that he was almost rubbing his hands together with glee.

"The wealthy merchants' sons, they're always trying to outdo one another – all except Mr Morton that is – he has no need to outdo anyone, he's the wealthiest of the lot. If any of the others hear of this, they'll likely come looking to buy something similar – so I hope you've got some quality work for me."

Silently, Serafine placed her basket on the counter, and lifted out her latest work.

There were 5 favours, each unique, some heart shaped, some not, made using a mixture of ordinary ribbon and lace, and some of the unusual bits and pieces she'd bought from the fashionable shop.

"I think that these would please the most exacting customer. I will have to ask you for a slightly higher price for these, Mr Tanner – for the materials are a bit more expensive – but if you want to tempt the wealthy, the items have to be of a suitable quality."

She waited, outwardly looking calm, serene, but inwardly terrified that he would refuse to pay extra. He looked closely at the favours, obviously wanting them, unconsciously narrowing his eyes in that characteristic expression of avarice. Eventually he looked up.

"I do agree Miss, things need to be obvious quality to sell to the better class of customer. I like these – I'll give you a better price."

Serafine nearly sagged from relief. And so the haggling commenced – for Mr Tanner couldn't agree to anything without some haggling. When they were done, Serafine was happy, for she had secured his agreement to a standard price twenty percent higher than that which he had paid for her previous work. Mr Tanner looked happy too – so she suspected that she could have pushed him for more, and succeeded. But haggling was exhausting – at least they were both happy with this outcome.

Now that she could stop worrying about the money, something of what he had said earlier came back to Serafine.

Surely that richest merchant family he had mentioned — Morton wasn't it? Surely she'd heard that name recently? Then it came to her, a clear little bubble of memory in her mind. The old woman in the other shop — she'd said she bought from Morton Empire Imports — it had to be owned by the family Mr Tanner spoke of, for the chances of two wealthy merchant families of the same name were low. Taking a deep breath, she spoke as casually as she could.

"This Mr Morton you mentioned — the wealthiest merchant? What does his business do, that they are so wealthy?"

Mr Tanner was always happy to show off his knowledge of everyone and everything, and especially when he could make himself look important by association. He puffed his chest up with that supposed importance, and launched into a long, gossipy explanation.

By the time he was done, Serafine knew all about the last two generations of Mortons, about how sad it was that the old man had died before his son Raphael returned from the war, how the son was a war hero, even if he didn't speak of it, how the mother was Italian, and her three children all strikingly good looking as a result, how young Mr Arbuthnot was sweet on Miss Isabella Morton, but Mr Tanner doubted he stood a real chance there, and she had also been treated to what seemed an exhaustive list of the sort of products that the firm imported, from the far reaches of the empire and beyond.

Her face and neck were aching from nodding and smiling as he talked and Serafine thought, with wry amusement, that she seemed to have developed rather a talent for gossiping with shopkeepers.

Taking advantage of a break in his conversation, she thanked him, and, escaped into the cold afternoon.

She was now absolutely certain that she needed to seek out the offices of Morton Empire Imports as soon as possible.

Chapter Five

Raphael rode through the streets, observing as the morning bustle gave way to quiet, the closer he came to Hyde Park. The *ton* did not rise early, unlike the merchants, even the wealthy merchants, who lived nearer his home. He felt the need to let his horse stretch out and shed its excess energy, to feel the wind on his face, to be moving.

His head was full of cobwebs and an ache that came from imbibing a little too much, yet he was happy – happier than he had been for many weeks. The previous evening he had, for the first time since their return, spent time with the rest of the Hounds, who were, with the start of the Season approaching, all in town. It had been wonderful – not just to see them, to feel at home again, in a way that he had deeply missed, but also because it had gone a long way to assuaging his fear of losing them.

He was still very cynical about their ability to continue to associate with him, as, should the *ton* become aware of it, they would most certainly show their disapproval pointedly.

But for now, all was well. He reached the park, and gave Foxfire his head. The rush of fresh air blew the last of the effects of the drink away, and the day was beautiful as the soft winter sun lit the frosted grass and trees in a sparkling glitter.

Two hours later, relaxed, and refreshed, he turned to make his way home, ready to tackle the day. He was preoccupied as he rode, still worrying at the challenge he had set himself before Christmas, to find a new project, which would leverage his existing stock, yet be unusual and attractive to the wealthy. It was proving a much bigger challenge than he had expected.

As he reached the Grosvenor gate, he was startled to see, perched on the high seat of a fashionable phaeton, his sister. She was laughing in delight as the young man beside her drove in through the gate at a rather indecorous pace. Who was Isabella with? He had not known that she intended to go out, and an early drive with a young man, with no more chaperonage than a very young looking tiger, who clung with some desperation to the back of the speeding vehicle, was not the sort of behaviour that he expected from her. He would not want her thought fast.

As they came closer, he realised that he knew the young man – it was, surprisingly, Porter Arbuthnot. His family had not been on good terms with the Arbuthnots for many years – not since his father's skilled handing of the business had brought them to wealth and prominence, quite eclipsing the Arbuthnots, who had, hitherto, been acclaimed as the wealthiest of merchants.

He wondered, as he moved aside, unnoticed by Bella and Arbuthnot, if this had been going on for any length of time.

Was Porter Arbuthnot courting Bella, seriously? Or was this merely an amusement to him? Or worse, some attempt at disadvantaging his family through disgracing his sister, in revenge for their mercantile success?

Raphael turned his horse, and followed them, at a distance, keeping amongst the trees and out on the grass, simply watching.

After a half hour or so, they turned back, and Raphael, relieved, followed as they proceeded, at a more sedate pace, through the streets towards his home. He had half expected them to stop in the park, and descend to walk in some secluded spot – which he could not have allowed.

As Arbuthnot deposited Bella at the front door of their home, Raphael slipped quietly into the lane at the rear, and delivered Foxfire to his groom. Striding into the house, he was in time to catch Bella still in the Hall, as she removed her fur pelisse and scarf.

"Is that the first time young Arbuthnot has taken you for a drive?"

Bella startled, her cheeks flushing a charming pink, which could charitably have been attributed to the cold wind outside, but which, to Raphael, more resembled guilt than anything else.

"N.. nnooo. It was the third time." Her voice had that edge of defiance that he recognised from many moments in her childhood. Her chin came up, and he could see that she was waiting for a reprimand. Intentionally choosing to disconcert her, he smiled genially.

"I would prefer, in future, that you have a maid with you, should you grant a gentleman the honour of taking you for a drive in the park. I would not have you thought fast, or your reputation called into question."

Obviously surprised, and expecting more, she glared at him for a moment.

"Yes Raphael, if you so insist."

It was too easy an acquiescence.

"Is he courting you? And do you wish it so?"

Bella flushed again, before half shaking her head. She answered with the honesty that was the essence of her, which endeared her to him more.

"I do not truly know. He is flattering, and amusing to be with. He flirts with me, but I am not sure that I would call it courting. I like it well enough, but... I am not sure if I wish it to become more."

Raphael did not allow his face to show the relief that he felt. A sudden insight made him ask, "Was it he who gave you that pretty Christmas favour?"

Bella nodded, blushing again, and said nothing more.

"Be careful Bella – best that you discover his true intentions before things go any further. After all, our families have been on less than friendly terms, ever since father began to do better than they, in business – it seems odd that he should be so friendly now.

She nodded again, and fled to her room to think.

Raphael went in search of a light meal, before turning his attention to the business of the day. Pensively, he considered the conversation with Bella, and, unbidden, the image of that Christmas favour rose in his mind again. He remembered her delight at receiving it, and their mother's admiration for its prettiness, as well as his own recognition, at the time, of the quality of its design.

Now there was a simple thing, which could yet be made in many different designs, which might interest the *ton*, as easily as it did his sister – so long as the quality of materials and manufacture was high enough. For the *ton* loved fripperies and extravagant gestures... the thought led to the very beginning of an idea.

<div align="center">~~~~~</div>

Serafine took a deep breath and pushed open the door, causing a bell attached to it to ring. Inside was a small seating area, and a counter, off to one side. Behind the counter, in an exquisitely constructed glass fronted case, were samples of fabrics, beads, feathers, and a range of other items. As she stood there, feeling nervous and unsure, the door to one side of the counter opened, and two men entered.

The first appeared to be a clerk, well dressed but ordinary. The second was another thing entirely. They were mid conversation as they entered, but stopped immediately upon noticing her presence. The second man turned towards her, taking her in with a single pass of his dark eyes, and she felt suddenly unable to breath, a flush of heat rushing through her entire body.

He was tall, lean and elegant, moving with the fluid economy that spoke of skill with weapons and military experience. His hair was dark, and his skin tanned as if from long exposure to the sun.

She thought that he looked somehow foreign, just a little – perhaps Italian? This must be Mr Morton - hadn't Mr Tanner said his mother was Italian?

She had never seen a man so handsome, so understated in his dress and manner, yet so utterly sure of himself.

He looked like he would have been completely at home in the ballrooms of the *ton* – yet, if he was here, and so obviously in a position of authority, if he was *the* Mr Morton, then he could not be of the nobility.

He waited, eyebrow raised, while she stood there, stunned to silence. When it became obvious that she was not about to speak, he approached her and asked, "Can I help you my Lady?"

She felt a ridiculous sense of relief, that she still looked enough of a Lady for him to grant her that status of address immediately. Would he still think her a Lady when she asked the questions she had come to ask?

"I hope so, Mr....?"

"Mr Raphael Morton, at your service, my Lady."

He swept a courtly bow over her hand, his eyes sparkling with some amusement.

"Welcome to Morton Empire Imports – how can we assist you today?"

Serafine's heart beat harder – she had not imagined the owner of such a large merchant business to be so young and good looking – somehow, she always expected successful merchants to be old, and bent from poring over ledgers.

"I… I would like to ask some questions about the materials that you import – to see if they may be suitable for a project of mine." Sera watched his reaction, hardly daring to breathe.

This was obviously not quite what he had expected her to say, but, being both a consummate gentleman, and a clever merchant, he simply waved her to the seating area and turned to the clerk.

"Jenkins, if you would, some tea and biscuits for Lady…. "

He looked at her enquiringly.

"Lady Serafine Parkington." She managed, just, to keep her voice steady as she spoke, waiting for the condemnation to appear in his eyes – for surely a merchant as wealthy as he would be aware of the gossip of the *ton*, would know of her disgrace.

He simply nodded, and waved Mr Jenkins on his way. She let out the breath that she had not realised she was holding, and lowered herself to a chair, depositing her basket on the floor at her side. He turned back to her.

"So, Lady Serafine, tell me more about your project, ask your questions, and let us see if I can supply what you wish for."

Wickedly, her internal voice suggested that he could supply many things that she wished for, in her most secret thoughts. She pushed it away, and began.

"First, Mr Morton, I must make an admission that may shock you, coming from a well born Lady."

At her words he looked most interested, and raised that enquiring eyebrow once again, but said nothing, waiting for her to continue.

"I... create... things. It began as a hobby of sorts, some years ago, but, in more recent times, it has become more... commercial... in nature. My family are in rather... straightened... circumstances, and I have been forced to supplement our income in small ways."

She waited, again, for an expression of horror or disgust to cross his face – for Ladies were not expected to sully themselves with work. It did not appear. He simply nodded, and she had the most peculiar feeling that, even wealthy as he was, he truly understood what it was to be poor.

At that moment, Jenkins returned with the tea tray, and placed it on a small table before them. She was forced to wait until Jenkins had left, and tea had been poured. It felt strange to have a man pour tea for her, but this was his premises, after all. At last she could continue.

"I am finding that I need more materials for my creations – materials of a better quality than those I have been able to source to date. It seems that there is a demand for my work – but a demand for items of the best materials. I only need very small amounts, as the items I make are quite small, but the materials must be unusual and high quality. I purchased some offcuts and other items from a shop selling trifles to Ladies of Quality, and the proprietress informed me that she purchases such things from your business. Hence my visit."

In her need to get her explanation out, Serafine had quite forgotten to be nervous, somewhere in the middle of speaking – perhaps because he seemed so genuinely interested in what she had to say. There was something about him that made her feel respected, safe, in a way that she had not, since… *before*. He appeared to consider for a moment, then spoke, his voice warm and positive, wrapping around her softly.

"It certainly sounds as if I may be able to assist you – but to do so, I believe that I will need to see an example of these items that you create, to better understand your needs. For I must confess, at this point I am at a loss to guess what they might be."

As he said it, she felt like a complete goose – how had she managed all of that long winded explanation, without ever actually telling him the core of it? She lifted her basket to her lap. Folding the cloth cover back, she lifted out the last of her most recently made favours, and, pushing aside the tea tray, laid them on the small table before them.

A small gasp escaped his lips, and he reached out a hand to lift one up and examine it, touching it as if it were some precious thing. She was not sure that her work deserved such reverence. Silently, she waited until he had completed his examination. When he looked to her again, his face was alight with what appeared to be excitement, with a smile that lit his eyes, and transformed him from merely handsome to utterly breathtaking.

"The perfect solution!" His exclamation confused her, and she waited for him to say more.

"Did you, perchance, make some of these just before Christmas, Lady Serafine? Including one with tiny holly berries and bells?"

She nodded, wondering how on earth he had seen it, when it had been purchased by that other merchant – Arbuthnot, if she remembered Mr Tanner's ramblings aright.

"Excellent! A hopeful swain gave it to my sister, and I was most impressed with its elegance and workmanship when I saw it. So was my mother, whose taste is quite beyond compare."

It was as if he had read her thoughts. She still could not fathom why he was so delighted, for surely the small amounts of materials that she might buy would be but the tiniest pittance compared to what most highborn Ladies might buy from him.

"Lady Serafine, I have a proposition for you." At the look of shock in her eyes, he gave a light laugh and continued, "A business proposition only, let me hasten to assure you, nothing of any impropriety, one which I most sincerely hope will be of monetary profit for both of us."

She found herself laughing with him, and a ridiculous, giddy bubble of hope was fluttering about in her chest. "Please, Mr Morton, you intrigue me – tell me more."

"I have been looking, this past month or more, for a new venture, a new way to use materials that I already have, or import often, to create something new to catch the interest of the *ton*. For the wealthy of Quality love to outdo each other with fripperies, and fads, and I would profit from that shallowness."

She nodded, fully understanding what he meant, for the outrageous fashions taken up by the *ton* had always both fascinated, and repelled, her even whilst she was one of them, and oblivious to how the world truly went on.

"Ever since I saw my sister's Christmas favour, it has niggled at the back of my mind – I felt it important, but did not know why. Now I do. For surely, this sort of thing, created with high quality materials and workmanship, and using exclusive, exotic imported materials would appeal to them. I need only gift a few select pieces to the current arbiters of fashion, or perhaps to the Prince Regent himself, and, should they like them, they will be all the rage overnight, and will be sent to young Ladies as often as hot-house flowers are."

Excitement shot through her, for this was her vision, multiplied tenfold. The thought that one day, a piece made by her hands, her, a shunned and disregarded member of society, might reach the hands of the Prince Regent was both satisfying and sublimely ridiculous. Still she must take care.

"That seems a wondrous concept, Mr Morton, yet... even with the best of materials, I can only make so many, for each takes some time. Should your vision come to pass, I could not keep up with such a demand."

Nervous again, she reached up from habit, tucking the escaped tendrils of her rich dark brown hair back. His eyes followed her movement, and she found herself caught in them. They simply looked at each other, until he broke the spell by speaking again.

"Ah, but I have a solution to that problem too."

Serafine was suddenly utterly conscious of everything around her, in fine detail – the colours of the fabrics on display, the subtle scent of oriental spices that pervaded the place, the pine and leather scent that could only be from Mr Morton himself, the muted sounds of movement in the back rooms of the shop. It was as if her future turned on this moment. She waited.

"It would be possible for you to teach others to make these, would it not?"

She nodded again.

"But… if I should do that, how would that make income for me?"

Perhaps her question sounded greedy, but she had to ask – her mother's survival, and her own, turned upon the answer.

"Because, Lady Serafine, you will not simply be a pair of hands to sew, you will be a business partner with me, and the business that you will own half of, will be a manufactory for these. I have a small building nearby that we can use, and we will employ poorer girls from hereabout, helping their families survive, and you will teach them how to make these to the exacting standards required for us to sell them to the *ton*. You will help me understand exactly how to make them something that the Ladies of the *ton* will crave – for of that world, you have much greater knowledge than I."

His eyes were alight with excitement again, and she found herself caught up in it, swept away by the scale of his idea. This was beyond all her imaginings. There was only one thing that she could do.

"Yes, Mr Morton, I accept your business proposition."

"Wonderful! We will need to move fast, for I believe that our best opportunity to launch this endeavour approaches. In but a month, it will be St. Valentine's Day, and people of all classes will be giving love tokens to those they admire. Can you design some suitable favours, that girls could make, in time for us to have them on sale before then?"

He was sweeping her along, and she felt like a leaf on a torrent, caught in the enthusiasm of his ideas. It was terrifying and exhilarating at once.

"I will most certainly do my best – but there is much to be done, and for some of it, I have no idea where to start, for I find that the education of a gently reared Lady is sadly lacking in the area of setting up a manufactory."

He laughed, delighted at her gentle wit, and reached to take her hands.

"My Lady, I will have a contract drawn up, immediately, so that you can be assured of your security in this enterprise. And I will arrange staff to assist you. If you will return here tomorrow morning at 10, all will be ready – you will have the contract, your staff, and the building at your disposal."

Stunned, she simply nodded, for the heat flowing through her from the touch of his hands quite fuddled her brain, his nearness leaving her more flustered than that of any man, ever before. He looked at her again, as if considering whether he should speak further. Then, apparently, he decided that he should.

"I will understand should you be offended at what I am about to say, but I feel that I must say it, nonetheless."

The old dread curled in her – was she, after such a wonderful few minutes, about to meet the rejection again – had he, perchance, just remembered the scandal attached to her name?

"I sense, Lady Serafine, in what you said, and what you did not say, that your financial position is, at present, very difficult? I must commend you for your initiative in acting to change that, for many young women of the aristocracy would simply retreat into tears and depression, and starve."

She could do nothing but nod, again (he must be beginning to wonder if she had a weak neck, for she had been nodding stupidly through half of this conversation!). She was embarrassed at the truth of his words about her poverty, yet elated to find that he actually respected her for taking action. It was a novel experience for a man to regard her that way. When he continued, it was tentative, as if he expected her to push him away. Startled, she realised that he still held her hands.

"Lady Serafine, in recognition of the enormous effort that you have agreed to put in, over the next weeks, before our enterprise will begin to make sales, I wish to offer you an amount now – an amount that I regard as being fair compensation for the licensing of your idea and knowledge, for use in this business. Can you see your way to accept such a thing?"

She understood his concern, for a 'true Lady' would reject such apparent charity with scorn.

She was long past such scruples.

'Mr Morton, that is a more than generous offer, in the light of all that you have already agreed to do, and to contribute to this business. But, I am somewhat embarrassed to admit, you have assessed it correctly. My situation is somewhat dire. So, for my mother's sake, I will most gratefully accept your offer, in the spirit it is made."

"You, Lady Serafine, exhibit great courage and sense, as well as beauty. I cannot imagine a better person as a business partner!"

After a short further conversation, which she barely managed, so dazed was she by the fact that he spoke of her as beautiful, as she was about to turn and leave, he shook her hand, just as if she were another gentleman of business!

Then he drew forth a purse and handed it to her, saying quietly, "An advance, Lady Serafine – I will have a draft on my bank for you tomorrow, along with everything else. But I do not wish to see you in any difficulty. Please, take a hackney home, for your safety - it grows dark."

"Thank you." What more could she possibly say?

All the way home she replayed the afternoon in her mind, hugging it to her as if it might dissolve in the winter rain outside. But the purse was real, as was the scent of Mr Morton, which clung to her hands where he had held them, and seeped, dizzyingly, into her senses.

Raphael watched her leave, feeling at once bemused, confused and more excited and alive than he had since arriving home from the war. She was a stunning woman – rich dark brown hair, thick and a little unruly, curling into tendrils from the winter damp, eyes that were almost golden, that seemed to glow from within when she was caught up in an idea, a figure that no worn and slightly outdated dress could hide, and lips that should, oh definitely should, be kissed.

And she was intelligent, resourceful and loyal. It was a seemingly impossible combination, but, improbable as it was, it existed. His friends might think him mad, but he had no doubts about the decisions he had just so impetuously made. He was quite, quite certain, with the instinct that had kept him alive in Spain, that she was everything she said she was, and that this would work.

And, he had to admit to himself, the thought of days with a woman like that, to create a new venture, was arousing – in more than one way – he would not at all object to spending time working with such a beautiful woman at his side.

Chapter Six

That night, Serafine slept better than she had for months. Her sleep was threaded through with dreams of Mr Raphael Morton, whose handsome face and compelling dark eyes seemed even more so in dreams. The purse he had handed her was under her pillow, and the subtle remnants of his personal scent which clung to it surrounded her.

The money it had contained was safely locked in her little metal box, along with the heart of lace which had begun all of this. She had been astonished, when, upon reaching home, she had dared to investigate just what the purse contained. More than thirty pounds! Enough to keep them, in their current excessively frugal lifestyle, for months! And this was his idea of a small 'advance' on what he intended to pay her for agreeing to join him in a business venture! A venture which would, later, also return her a share of the profits!

It all seemed too good to be true, yet she knew that it was true. She had never felt more certain of a man's honesty and good intentions in her life.

Her mother had been abed when she had returned, and she had not disturbed her. Now, as the weak morning sun shone through her somewhat grimy bedroom window, she rose and dressed, eager to tell her mother of the momentous events of the day before.

In their little breakfast room, they sat to a plain repast of bread, cheese and a little cold meat. Serafine ate, then, unable to wait any longer, she began.

"Mother, I have such news! Wonderful news. News which, it is my hope, will solve our precarious financial situation forever."

Her mother looked up, startled, and was overjoyed to see the light in her daughter's eyes, and the enthusiasm in her expression – neither of which had been present since her brother's death. As Serafine went on to explain, her mother's face showed at first doubt and uncertainty, but swiftly moved to a hope equal to Serafine's. When Sera spoke of the funds already received, her mother's amazement and relief were obvious, although deeply coloured by embarrassment at having their severe financial straits known.

"This Mr Morton sounds a positive paragon – you are quite certain that he is being honest with you? That he will not try to take advantage of you in… inappropriate ways?"

"Quite certain – he is everything a gentleman should be – much more so than many of those young rakes and fops of the *ton*, who panted after me, then were the first to turn away."

"I would meet him. Might I accompany you this morning, to see that all is in order, and set my mind at ease?"

Serafine was most glad of her mother's interest – it had been many months since her mother had set foot outside their house, her depression had been so deep.

"Why certainly mother, if you will not be embarrassed to be seen about without a maid to accompany us."

"As we have no maid, I will have to be content, will I not? You have seemed to do well enough in these circumstances Sera, much though such things might once have horrified me."

Both smiling, they rose from the table and went to prepare for the day.

~~~~~

From the moment she had walked out his door, Raphael had swept into action, summoning his man of business to draw up the contract, arranging staff to be allocated to support of this new project, and sending Jenkins to arrange a cleaning of the building they would use, which had recently come into his possession as payment of a debt from a Lord who was financially embarrassed at present, but whose wife had spent rather excessively on the silks that Raphael imported.

He fell into a deep sleep, late in the night, and woke with the dawn, feeling full of energy. For the first time since his return, there was no trace of boredom in his thoughts. After Garrett had assisted him with dressing (a situation he still found peculiar after years at war, looking after himself), and he had broken his fast, he gathered up his hat and gloves, and slipped on his caped winter coat.
~~~~~

As he turned to the door, Bella came down the stairs, just beginning her day. He went to her and took her hand a moment.

"Bella, dear sister, I must thank you."

She looked at him, startled at this pronouncement.

"You see, dear sister, that pretty Christmas favour you showed me, it has given me a new business idea, which I hope to find most profitable. I shall tell you more this evening, but for now, my thanks."

He swept on his way before she could do anything but smile. It was typical of Raphael, she thought, to leave her with a tiny bit of information, and expect her to wait all day to hear more!

~~~~~

At precisely the hour of ten, the door to Morton Empire Imports opened, and Lady Serafine entered, followed, Raphael was surprised to see, by an older woman. A woman who could only be her mother, he thought, for the resemblance was clear. The older woman's hair was streaked with some grey, but was still thick and shining, and the sharp lines of her high cheekbones were a clear echo of the softer lines of Lady Serafine's face.

Raphael bowed over their hands.

"Lady Serafine. And this is…?'

"My mother, the Dowager Lady Galwood."
~~~~~

For a moment, as she spoke, fear flickered across Serafine's face, and that of her mother also. More than a year of being treated to the cut direct, as soon as people discovered who they were, had left its mark. Raphael wondered at the fleeting expression, but let that go to think about later.

"Delighted, my Lady. I am Mr Raphael Morton, owner of Morton Empire Imports. Your daughter is most talented and enterprising. I count myself fortunate to have found such a person to be my partner in this business venture."

He waved them to the seating area.

"Please be seated, I will have everything brought momentarily. Might I offer you some refreshment? Some tea, perhaps?"

"Thank you, Mr Morton." Lady Galwood was, suddenly, the elegant aristocratic woman that Sera remembered, rather than the shadow that she had lived with for the last year.

By the time another hour had passed, Serafine was in possession of a signed contract, making her the half owner of a new business, to be called Parkmorton Gifts, a signed bank draft for a remarkable amount of money, a business manager in the form of Mr Jenkins, who had agreed to take on this new challenge, a housekeeper in the form of Mrs Jenkins, who would assist with hiring domestic staff, as well as finding girls to employ in the manufactory, as she was well known in the surrounding area, and an assistant, a Miss Emily Nunn, who would help with identifying suitable materials from the vast stores of exotic items in Morton Empire Imports warehouses.

Once again, she felt like a leaf tossed on the torrent.

It was wonderful, exhilarating and positively the most frightening experience of her life. Her mother appeared to feel the same way, as she watched all of this happen with amazement.

There followed a visit to their new building, which was only a few blocks away, where Sera could barely contain her excitement – for it was large, larger than she had ever imagined, and, whilst still being cleaned after some time unused, was most suitable, with rooms for offices, sitting rooms for meetings, a tidy kitchen, storerooms, and a selection of large rooms with excellent windows where the light would be suitable for girls to sit and do the fine sewing necessary.

There was also a small stable at the rear, where the yard opened onto a lane between the buildings. And… the stable contained a small town carriage, two horses, and a cheerful groom/coachman named Alf. Mr Morton casually informed Sera that they were for her use – she was now an important merchant, and should look the part, apparently.

At the end of the visit, when Mrs Jenkins had arrived and been introduced, Alf drove Lady Galwood and Mrs Jenkins back to Sera's home, to begin on the hiring of staff and the planning there, and Sera returned to Morton Empire Imports office with Mr Morton, and Mr Jenkins, to begin planning in earnest.

By evening she was elated, and exhausted, and still only just beginning to believe that this was real. The sense of unreality was heightened when she reached home (driven by Alf!) and a footman opened the door for her.

Mrs Jenkins greeted her in the hall, and introduced the shy locking young girl standing behind her as, "Polly, your new maid, my Lady."

As she dropped into sleep that night, the thought drifted through her mind that it was incongruous, and rather amusing, that the thing that should give her back something almost like her old life was to 'sully her hands with trade' – that idea most reviled by the nobility. After a year of barely surviving, she would take practical and comfortable over poverty and ridiculous concepts of noble behaviour every time.

~~~~~

Over dinner that evening, Raphael had, as promised, explained his new venture to Bella, and the rest of his family. His mother thought it an excessively clever idea, and praised his astuteness in capturing Lady Serafine's skills before anyone else saw the potential. Gabriel thought it boring – girls sewing fripperies held no interest for him – he would rather listen to the sea captain's tales of exotic lands.

Bella thought it wonderful, and romantic, that making love tokens should transform the life of a woman fallen on difficult times, as well as make what should be the coup, for their own business, of starting a new fashion. Perhaps she would tell Porter Arbuthnot what a wonderful chain of events his gift of the favour had set in motion.

She was still unsure how she felt about him, but she had agreed to another drive tomorrow, albeit insisting that it be in a vehicle where Liza, her maid, could accompany them.
~~~~~

Indulging in a quiet glass of port with his mother, after the meal was done, Raphael was surprised when she spoke, breaking into his thoughts of business.

"Raphael, Lady Serafine… you said that her mother is the Dowager Lady Galwood?"

"Yes, that was the name." He wondered where this conversation was going.

"I seem to remember something about that name. From more than a year ago, whilst you were still at war. Before your father…"

Her voice caught, for she still missed her husband fiercely, although she rarely let that show. He waited, sipping his port, letting the stresses of the hectic day slide away, as she paused, seemingly sifting through memories. Eventually, she spoke again.

"I remember now. There was a scandal, young Viscount Galwood, that would be Lady Serafine's brother, killed himself. Gambling debts, I believe. He had gambled away everything not entailed, and left his family ruined, so he took the coward's way out and killed himself. His mother and sister were cut dead by the *ton*, for the scandal of having a suicide in the family, and the title went to some distant cousin. That would explain their straightened circumstances, and her need to create an income."

"Whilst I cannot see that suicide should ever be a choice for a man of any class with any honour, I also cannot see why the *ton* must cast aside the family of such a man. Surely they suffer enough in losing him, without needing disgrace added to that."

"Raphael, I must agree with that sentiment. The poor women, this last year must have been hell. It does, however, amaze me that this Lady Serafine has the vision and the courage to have even considered working, and going into business – for most members of the *ton* would surely actually starve before they did so!"

"She is, indeed, most unusual." As Raphael spoke, the image of her rose in his mind, as she had been that morning, flushed, excited at what they had begun, golden eyes alight, rich dark hair escaping its pins to lie in tendrils around her face, and full of intelligent questions. She was beautiful in an unconventional kind of way, for he found that her beauty came as much from her keen intelligence as from her fairness of form.

He also remembered, in that instant, the fleeting expression that had crossed both Lady Serafine's and her mother's countenance – could it have been fear? Did they fear that he would act as the *ton* did, and reject them for the actions of her brother, actions over which they, personally, would have had no influence whatsoever?

With him, they had no need for fear, he would never behave that way. But… he wondered, how the other Hounds would respond? They were of the *ton* (although Gerald had only recently risen to such high estate), would they reject her? Or see it as he did? It was the first time that he had ever had to consider a situation where their opinions might be so divided. He did not like the possibility at all.

"Thank you for the information, Mother, I will bear that in mind as we proceed with this."

Soon after, he took himself to bed, to dream of golden eyes and hair the colour of rich mahogany timber from the East Indies.

Chapter Seven

Two days later, whilst Serafine and Raphael were immersed in a whirlwind of arranging the manufactory, hiring girls, choosing materials and starting to teach them how to make the favours, Isabella was nervously awaiting the arrival of Mr Porter Arbuthnot, her maid, Liza, standing patiently by her side.

When she saw, peering through the curtains of the front parlour, the small but elegant open carriage draw up outside, Isabella breathed a sigh of relief – she hated waiting... for anything.

A moment later, there was a knock on the door, and the footman ushered Mr Arbuthnot in.

"Miss Isabella, you are beautiful as always." He took her hand, and performed an exaggerated bow, his lips barely brushing her glove. Liza stifled a giggle. Isabella glared at her, sidelong.

"Why thank you sir!"

He offered her his arm, and led her out to the carriage, Liza dutifully following. Once they reached the park, and he could take some of his attention from the task of avoiding collisions, he asked her how she had been, declaring that he had missed her terribly since they had last met. Isabella blushed, not entirely convinced, but certainly flattered.

"Why Mr Arbuthnot, I believe you are gulling me. For, surely, your duties in your father's business must occupy your thoughts the majority of the time?"

"Ah Miss Isabella, nothing can completely distract me from thoughts of you." She was beginning to find his approach rather overdone, now that she considered it. Still, perhaps he was sincere.

"Well… I have mostly been rather bored, for it has been a little too cold for my liking, to walk, or even to visit my friends. Still, I do have one bit of news that may please you. You remember, I am sure, that delightful Christmas favour you gave me?"

He looked at her, puzzled by this turn in the conversation, and nodded.

"Well, it was so beautiful that I showed it to my family at the time. My mother, and my brother, both thought it most elegant and well made – a very nice sentiment. And now I find that it has inspired my brother to a new enterprise. He plans to arrange the making of such things, to sell through our business! Your romantic gesture has resulted in good fortune for us, and for a Lady who has agreed to assist with this venture. Isn't that wonderful!"

Whilst Isabella was enamoured of the romantic nature of the whole concept, it seemed to her that Mr Arbuthnot was not. As she spoke, it had seemed to her, for a moment, that an expression of annoyance, almost anger, had crossed his face – but... surely not? For what was there, in what she had said, that might conceivably annoy him?

After that, for the rest of their drive, whilst he spoke most amiably to her, he seemed a little distracted, and flattered and flirted considerably less than usual – a development that Isabella was not sure she appreciated at all. Still it was a pleasant outing, and she returned home happy enough with the day.

~~~~~

Two sennights later, Sera regarded the shelves of the storeroom with satisfaction. Neatly laid out, each wrapped in a delicate bag of sheerest muslin, the shelves contained the first 200 favours of their manufacture. Ten girls now worked for her each day, and they were proving most adept at learning the required skills to produce very high quality favours.

The selection of exquisite silk ribbons, fine laces, beads of exotic woods and metals and highest quality paste gems which had been chosen from the warehouses of Morton Empire Imports had proved of perfect suitability to bring the designs that she had envisaged to life. Tomorrow, Raphael... Mr Morton, she sternly corrected herself... intended to send a selection of the best favours to the Prince Regent, and one or two of the *ton's* most acknowledged arbiters of fashion.
~~~~~

The thought of it was both immensely satisfying and utterly terrifying – for what if they did not take the fancy of these important people?   Then all of this work might be for nought, and, if their venture did not succeed, what would become of her income, or the income that this work now provided for the girls?

Raphael had taken the ones that he had selected to his home, to sit, this evening, and write carefully crafted letters to accompany the gifts. Now, all was quiet. She had sent the girls home, with her enthusiastic thanks for their hard work so far, and was, as she usually did, taking a bit of quiet time to herself, tidying things away, and assuring herself that all was well, and ready for the next day.

She had locked the doors, all but the little one at the rear, and sat, now, appreciating the peace, still astounded at her good fortune, and at how much the last weeks had changed her life. All because one man had chosen to listen to her, had seen the potential in her idea, and, rather than simply stealing it from her, had given her the great gift of treating her as he might another man, and taking her on as a business partner.

He was a remarkable man.   She found herself wool-gathering, dreaming of him – his deep dark eyes, his lean elegant face, his strong hard body and his voice that flowed over her like a rich wine. As if that wasn't enough, he was a good and kind person. So much for the disdain that the *ton* held for those of the merchant class! Her experience with Mrs Johnson and the other ladies had begun the change in her view of the world, but Mr Raphael Morton had quite totally turned those views upside down.

If she was completely honest with herself, she was half in love with the man. Which was riciculous – to him, she was a business partner, nothing more. He insisted on treating her with the full deference due to a Lady of Quality, no matter her circumstances. She felt it like a wall between them – no matter how they might speak of the business, and converse freely and happily, it was as if the invisible barrier of the difference in their birth grew stronger over time, not weaker.

It saddened her, yet she supposed it was the way of the world.

~~~~~

Raphael sat back, shaking the sand from the last carefully penned letter. Leaving it aside for the ink to completely dry, he turned to the small stack of boxes on the side table, and began to pack the favours carefully into each, counting them as he did so. After three checks of his count, he huffed a frustrated breath. There was one too few. He had been a fool, and allowed himself to be distracted by watching the afternoon sun draw deep red lights from Sera's... Lady Serafine's, he corrected himself... beautiful hair and had miscounted when collecting the favours.

There was nothing for it. This had to be perfect.

He locked the door to his study, collected his hat and coat from the footman on duty at his door and set out to walk the moderate distance back to the manufactory, to select the final required favour.
~~~~~

~~~~~

Some sound brought Sera out of her dreaming, and she flushed, a little embarrassed at having been mooning over a man like a love-struck young girl. Glancing around, she realised that more time had passed than she had thought – the windows showed only the deepening dusk outside - her mother would be expecting her home. It was odd, though – normally Alf would have come to find her by now, keen to drive her home before it got too late and cold. She wondered where he was.

A sound came again, and an odd, reddish light tinted the dusk through the window. Alarmed, she stood, and ran to look. From the window she saw, to her horror, the flickering light of flames – she ran to the rear door, and went to open it, but the heat of the metal door handle nearly burnt her palm, and she backed away in fear. She grabbed for her keys and ran to the front of the building, through the small kitchen.

Her skirt caught on the logs waiting near the kitchen hearth, and she was spun by the tug, the keys flying from her hands and down into the grated drain near the washtub under the small window. She froze, staring at where they had disappeared, terror taking hold deep inside her. She had seen what fire could do to houses, had seen people barely rescued in time from a burning building. At that instant, she saw her death before her.

She could hear the fire now, burning the door, and the window frames – she ran, again.
~~~~~

Perhaps she could force open a window at the front, and attract some passer-by's attention. But the windows were all secure, with strong bars – they had put great effort into protecting this property, and their new venture. Despairing, she crumpled to the floor against the front door, then shook herself out of the stupor, and pulled a pin from her hair. She had heard tales of hairpins being used to pick locks – this was the time for her to attempt such a feat, if ever.

Three blocks from the manufactory, a rough looking man stepped out of the shadows, and approached the well-dressed young gentleman who stood in the pool of dim light from a nearby street lantern.

"It be done, just like ye wanted. Ye can see the colour from here." He pointed and, indeed, the red flicker of light from flames was visible on the wall of a tall building some distance away. The rough man held out his hand, and, unspeaking, the young gentleman deposited a heavy purse upon it.

"Always happy to oblige, Mr Porter, if'n ye should need me again." He sketched a parody of a formal bow, turned, and faded into the shadows.

The young gentleman stood a while longer, watching the colour on the wall, then nodded to himself, turned and was gone.

Raphael took the shorter way to the manufactory, ducking through the lanes to the rear, in a hurry to get the favour and get home, to have all in readiness for the morrow. He turned the last corner and stopped in shock for a second, before launching himself forward at a full run. For the back wall of the manufactory was wreathed in flame, and the yellow and red tendrils of it were licking towards the stable.

Surely Sera and Alf were both safe, for by now Alf should be driving her home, but he would not let all of their work be destroyed – not when they were so close to a great success!

He reached the stables and ran inside, grabbing a horse blanket from the rack and soaking it in the horse trough at the door, then used the wet wool to beat out the flames which were just reaching the stable wall, carried on the few wisps of spilled hay and straw that had not been swept up – he thanked the Lord God that they kept a neatly swept yard at all times. As Raphael turned to thrust the blanket into the trough again, he heard a moan from inside the stable.

He glanced at the door, then at the manufactory building – the flames were gaining strength – he had little time, but... if that was Alf, he needed help. And, if that was Alf, could it be that Sera was still inside? His heart beat harder than it ever had in his life, and horror froze him to the spot. Then his battle reflexes took over, and the judgement honed on the field of war took him into a cold calm space where he assessed his options in an instant, and acted.

As Raphael turned to the stable door, Alf staggered out, unsteady on his feet, and clutching his head. His face, already white, turned ashen when he saw the flames.

Alf pointed, shaking, and croaked in a harsh voice "Lady Serafine...."

In that moment, Raphael was utterly grateful for the cold calm of battle, for under it, he felt fear greater than ever before – fear of losing a woman that he had come to care for, well beyond the respect a man might have for a skilled business partner. Despite the difference in their stations in Society, she had, in these last few sennights, become central to his life.

Grabbing the soaked horse blanket, he threw himself at the building like a madman, beating at the flames. Moments later, water splashed past him to land at the base of the flames where grass and straw, and a scatter of refuse reeds from the kitchen floor gave the fire enough fuel to keep it hot on the timber of the door. Alf turned and was soon back with another bucket full.

Raphael beat at the higher flames, spending all of his effort to stop it spreading further, working along the wall as best he could, and desperately wishing for more hands to help. He kicked aside the neatly piled stack of logs kept for the kitchen fire, scattering them into the icy slush of the yard, satisfied that they would not burn further there. The blanket began to burn, and he ran back to the water trough to soak it again.

As he did, three young men rushed past him into the yard, buckets in hand, and a small spark of hope filled him. With extra hands, they had a chance. A fraught fifteen minutes later, the fire was out. The rear door and window frame were nearly burnt away, the window broken, and all of the mortaring of the stone of the wall would need redoing, but the building stood.

His elegant clothes charred and blackened with soot, Raphael stood a moment, quickly bowed, and thanked the young men, then threw himself at the door, breaking through what remained of the still smouldering timber. His three young assistants looked at Alf quizzically, as if to ask if the man was mad. Alf shook his head, and again, pointed.

"Lady Serafine."

Horrified comprehension spread across the faces of the men.

"No… She give me sister a job there, we'd be close to starving without that – we came to help because a' that. I nivver thought the Lady might be trapped."

Alf just waited, quietly praying. He had faith in Mr Morton. But what if Lady Serafine was hurt… or worse?

Chapter Eight

Sera struggled with the hairpin, but the lock was stubborn, and her fingers began to hurt from the effort of trying. At first, apart from the fear, it was not so bad – this far from the back of the building, there was no heat, but she could hear the flames, hear cracks and thumps as the building suffered its assault. But, after a few minutes, there was a loud cracking noise, and a tinkle of falling glass. The kitchen window must have shattered in the heat.

That was enough to start a flow of air into the building – air laden with thick smoke. As the smoke began to fill the rooms, Sera coughed and struggled to breathe, to concentrate on the lock – surely she could manage to pick it! But it stubbornly refused to open. And she began to feel light headed, her vision blurring as the smoke made her eyes shed continuous tears.

It was no good, she thought despairingly. She had tried so hard. That everything she had worked for should end like this, and her with it, was insupportable. But it was happening.

She sagged against the front door, barely able to breathe any more, and wished desperately that she might see her mother to say goodbye, that she might see Raphael, to tell him how she felt about him – whether it be foolish of her or not. But that was a fever dream – the reality was the darkness closing in and the air no longer supporting her breath.

Just as she slipped into the blackness, she thought she heard a resounding crash – surely her exit from this life was not to be announced with a clash of drums? Then there were arms around her, and she was lifted against a hard chest, which was surely real, for she could feel it move as its owner coughed in the smoke filled room.

Moments later, sweet fresh air filled her lungs, and, subtly underlying it, she recognised the pine and leather scent that could only mean that it was Raphael who held her so tightly against him, even as he staggered a little, passing through the burnt doorway and into the yard. It seemed that her prayer had been answered. He staggered as far as the stable, still holding her, and collapsed on the bench just inside.

Sera opened her eyes, to find his only inches away. A magical stillness overcame them both, and everything else but his eyes seemed to fade away. She had never seen anything so wonderful in her life.

"Sera." His voice was a smoked strained croak, but her name on his lips was sweet nonetheless – for no-one but her mother usually called her Sera, not since James…. And then those lips were upon hers and a sweet heat rushed through her body. She felt alive, intensely so, most especially because, short minutes ago, she had expected death.

After some unfathomable length of time, the kiss stopped, and they found themselves simply gazing at each other.

"Raphael…" her voice was a smoke shattered whisper, but he heard in his heart what she had no voice to say. He pulled her tight against him.

"Alf…"

"Yes, Mr Morton?"

Alf stuck his head around the door, looking pleased when he saw her still in Raphael's arms, but with her eyes open and obviously not badly hurt.

"Please arrange with the helpful young men outside to have a guard mounted on the building until we can arrange repairs tomorrow. They will be amply rewarded. And then, if the horses are alright, please hitch them up – I think that we will need the carriage to take Lady Serafine home."

"Yes, Sir!"

Once Sera was safely settled in the carriage, Raphael stepped back.

"One moment – there is one more thing that I must do, before we are on our way."

He turned and went back into the building, making his way carefully to the storeroom, and selected the one extra favour that he had come for. And a blessing it was that he had miscounted to start with – for had he not, Sera might now be dead, and all their work in ashes. The thought that he might have lost her was a band of agony on his heart.

Climbing into the carriage, and meeting her enquiring expression, he explained, in his roughened voice, just how he had come to be there, to save her.

She was beginning to think that the favours were the signposts of change in her life. What might they bring to her next?

Chapter Nine

For the first time in a very long while, Raphael was nervous. It was an odd sensation, and not a comfortable one. He had seen the carefully and elegantly wrapped boxes, each containing a number of the Saint Valentine's Day themed favours, and a carefully penned letter, dispatched for individual delivery by footmen in his employ, each dressed in new and impressive livery. Now there was nothing but waiting – for the men's return, and then for the reaction of the recipients.

He turned the nervous energy to good effect, and set about arranging the repairs to the building, so that business might go on as before. He had arrived to find that the young men had been true to their word, and diligently guarded the manufactory overnight. He handed each of them a sizeable purse, and sent them off home to rest. They were effusive in their gratitude, but he brushed it aside, assuring them that their efforts in helping him fight the fire, and then as guards, were worth that and more.

As he settled the last of the girls to working, and saw the last of the workmen off to obtain the required repair materials, he was surprised when Sera arrived. He had expected her to spend today recuperating from her experience – but obviously she was made of sterner stuff. He was unreasonably pleased to discover that to be the case.

He was not sure how to approach her – he had kissed her yesterday, and she had most certainly not pushed him aside, yet today, it was as if nothing, and yet everything, had changed between them. Did she regret that kiss now, in the light of a new day? Did she think it presumptuous that he, a merchant, should have kissed a Lady born? He certainly did not regret his actions, and if truth be told, he would happily sweep her into his arms immediately, and kiss her again. But all of his training made him wait to see her reaction, for he was utterly unsure of how she might respond.

So he held himself back, drinking her in with his eyes, seeing just how beautiful she was, and feeling again that sense of how lucky he was not to have lost her. He bowed, allowing himself to take her hand.

"My Lady, I am surprised, and very glad, to see you looking so well today. I had feared that your terrible experience yesterday might have left you less than well today."

A brilliant smile lit her face, and she shook her head.

"Oh no Mr Morton, I will not let such a thing prevent me from being here – for we must not let this stop us. This venture must succeed, and I fully intend to be here to do my utmost to ensure that. Even if my voice is frightfully unmelodic at this point."

It was true that her voice still suffered from the effects of the smoke, but he found the low, slightly roughened tone of it seductive, indeed, almost erotic, rather than unpleasant in any way. She flushed a little, as if suddenly unsure how to go on with him, and turned away, going to each of the girls in turn, to reassure them of their continued employment and to see to their work in progress.

Feeling suddenly unnecessary, Raphael turned away, and took himself home, hoping that his deliveries had, by now, all been made.

~~~~~

All but one of the footmen had returned, and reported that each parcel had been received with curious interest, delivered, as per his instructions, only directly into the hands of the persons he had so carefully selected as his targets. The one who had not yet returned had been tasked to deliver his parcel to the Prince Regent – a challenge which, it was entirely possible, might take him days to achieve.

Raphael could not settle to anything, and found himself prowling the house like a caged tiger, looking for something to distract him from the tension of the waiting. There was no point him going to his offices, for he would only disturb his perfectly efficient shop and warehouse staff, yet simply waiting would drive him quite mad. He entered the parlour, and discovered Bella, curled inelegantly in a chair, a book in her hand – a book it was quite obvious she was not actually reading.
~~~~~

Upon his arrival, Bella heaved a dramatic sigh. Raphael repressed his amusement, and, instead, asked her casually, "What causes you to sigh so, dear sister?"

"Oh Raphael! I am so bored. For this last sennight, Mr Porter Arbuthnot has not seen fit to invite me for a drive. I may not be entirely sure that I desire his interest, but at least he has provided me with some amusing conversation, and the chance to get out. And now he has abandoned me! Not even a message for days!"

"Perhaps, Bella, he feels that you have not shown any great interest in him, and has decided to not press his attentions if you do not wish him to?"

"But… surely any man who truly cared for me would not be so easily discouraged?"

"Perhaps you have simply confused him, then?"

"You are no help at all!" Bella dropped the book onto the table at her side, with rather more force than was seemly. Watching her, amused, yet sympathetic, he decided to act.

"Bella, if you so wish to go for a drive in the park, I shall take you. For I find myself with some free time this afternoon." She spun to him, a smile claiming her face.

"Raphael! That is most kind of you. Yes, I would love to go for a drive, please, may we go now?"

Nodding his agreement, he led her from the room.

When the final footman had returned, it was to report his mission a success – he had actually managed to deliver the parcel into the hands of the Prince Regent himself. It seemed that fortune had favoured him, for, as the footman had made his request for audience, he had been overheard by Cecil Carlisle, Baron Setford, who had, at mention of Raphael's name as the sender, turned back a moment, and whispered something to the Prince Regent. Suddenly, the footman had been waved forward, and given the chance to deliver the elaborately presented favours.

Raphael was elated – for if the favours were a success, orders would follow. He did wonder, in passing, what Setford had said. He had not seen the man since leaving the military, yet he suspected that Setford would be aware of his movements still.

Within the day, the whispers of gossip began to make their way back to him, reported faithfully by his employees and household staff – for many of them had sisters and brothers, or other relatives and friends, working in the houses of the nobility. For a merchant, the gossip was valuable, and allowed him to most effectively supply the desires of his highest paying customers.

But this time, the gossip was newly precious, for it told of the progress of the favours. Being items designed to be given, those he had sent them to were now doing exactly that – giving them to the women they admired. It seemed that Ladies of all stations had received them, from actresses to the daughters of the nobility. And, most pleasing of all, the current most favoured mistress of the Prince Regent.

Although this was what Raphael had intended, it was succeeding faster than he had expected. By the following day, he heard of shopkeepers in Bond Street receiving enquiries from members of the *ton*, who were seeking to purchase these newly fashionable favours, in time for the coming Saint Valentine's Day. Raphael, smiling, sent forth messengers again, this time bearing missives to all of the most exclusive shops, offering them the chance to obtain a supply of the favours – for a premium price, of course.

By the end of that day, they were sold out, and had a waiting list.

Chapter Ten

Serafine's life became a whirlwind of hiring and training more girls to make the favours, creating new designs, ensuring that everything was made to the best quality, packed and sent to the right addresses, occasionally remembering to eat, and falling into exhausted sleep each night. The success of the venture astounded her, and she was impressed at the cleverness with which Raphael had brought the favours to the attention of the *ton*.

Each time she saw him, her heart beat harder, her breath came a little short, and the memory of that kiss filled her mind. He was, to her, even more handsome and desirable when tired and somewhat dishevelled; carrying boxes along with his staff, being fully engaged in making sure that their venture was as successful as possible. She could not imagine any other gentleman she had met, of whatever station in Society, willingly doing such work. She certainly did not despise him for it, as convention said she should – indeed, she admired him instead.

After all, Society's mores said that she should also despise herself, for sullying her hands with work and trade. And that, she had long decided, was ridiculous – to have the funds to live in comfort, she was more than willing to work like this. A year of living in fading genteel poverty had impressed that on her, quite thoroughly.

They never touched, beyond the brief moment when he would gallantly greet her by bowing over her hand. She wished for more, but knew no way to breach the gulf that seemed to have opened between them. That kiss almost might not have been real, so distant, so unreachable did he seem now.

She had little time to think of it, however, except in the drifting moments before sleep took her each night, but it left her with a permanent little ache of sadness in her, nonetheless. Perhaps she had dreamed some of it – perhaps her smoke hazed brain had imagined the care in his voice when he had spoken her name, or the tenderness in his eyes when he had kissed her. She no longer knew what was real, beyond his presence every day, and the chaos of attempting to produce as many favours as the *ton* wished to buy.

~~~~~

Raphael ached. Somehow, he was fitting everything into the days – the running of Morton Empire Imports, the coordination of the distribution of the favours, making sure that Serafine was safe, that the building was repaired and guarded, and that everything that should happen, did happen, and nothing else.
~~~~~

He fell into bed each night, slept for not enough hours, and did it all again. He had not slept this little, and felt this worn, since Spain. Yet, at the same time, he revelled in it. For he was not bored, he was much too busy to feel trapped, as he had before, and everything that he did was succeeding, beyond his expectations.

There was, he had to admit, one thing that he was unhappy about. Serafine haunted his dreams, all golden eyes, pale skin and rich dark hair, soft in his arms, and pressing into his kiss. Over and over, he relived that moment in the stable – but only in dreams. He wished, with startling intensity, to make it more than dreams, but saw no way to do so. She was a Lady born, no matter that she chose now to engage herself in trade. He was not of her station. He might do business with her, but he could not expect to ever have her attentions in any other way.

Her family had suffered enough scandal – she did not need it added to, by an association with a merchant, beyond that of an astute investment in business. He would not do that to her. He was not certain, anyway, if she had truly, in any sense welcomed that kiss, or if her reaction at the time had only been the natural relief at finding herself alive, when she must have thought that her death was imminent.

So he watched her, his eyes drinking her in, his mind finding joy in her kindness and cleverness as she worked with the girls in the manufactory, transforming their lives, even as she transformed her own, his body aching to touch her, beyond that single touch he allowed himself each day – the torture of the moment when he greeted her and bowed over her hand.

He would never press his attentions on a woman who did not wish them – he had seen too much of the worst of that at war, so he suffered, not knowing if she even noticed him, beyond his existence as a business partner, and threw himself into the work to dull the pain.

And then, somehow, sennights had passed since the fire, and Saint Valentine's Day was upon them.

~~~~~

The last boxes were settled into the cart, and his delivery man drove off, keen to get them delivered and be done for the day. Raphael turned, wiping a hand across his brow, and stepped back into the building. Sera sat at the little kitchen table, her hands around a mug of slowly cooling tea.

They had sent all of the girls home, with a bonus payment each, and declared that the manufactory would be closed tomorrow. The day after that was Saint Valentine's Day – there was no more time to make and deliver favours for that day's benefit. What they made hereafter would be for other occasions.

Raphael sank into a chair opposite her, a sigh escaping his lips, to echo softly in the empty room. The silence, after so many days of busy work and voices, seemed wrong, deafening in its own way. Their eyes met, and time slowed. They sat, as the afternoon light faded into evening, simply drinking each other in, with no words said. It was a companionship of effort shared, and of words that neither dared speak.
~~~~~

In the end, it was Raphael who broke the spell. He stood, stretching a little, with the same grace and strength that a cat does, and held out his hand.

"Come Lady Serafine, let me drive you home. Your mother will be glad to see you, and the dark circles under your eyes tell me just how much you need to rest."

"Why Mr Morton," she smiled, "how every ungallant. A gentleman should never indicate that a Lady looks anything less than radiantly beautiful." That she had the energy left for even mild repartee after the last month astounded him, and yet was typical of her tenacious character.

But she took his hand, the first true touch they had shared since the kiss after the fire, and rose from the table to accompany him out the door. And he thought, as she did so, that to him, dark circles or no, she would always look radiantly beautiful.

He delivered her to her door, and accompanied her in, greeting Lady Galwood with genuine pleasure, seeing before him a changed woman, a woman restored to her rightful state of health and comfort. A woman who might not say so in words, but whose expression told him just as clearly how much she appreciated what her daughter, and Raphael, had done to transform her circumstances.

"Good Evening Lady Galwood. I fear that Lady Serafine has quite exhausted herself, and needs a day of rest. We have agreed to close the manufactory for tomorrow, so that all can rest after the hard work that has been done."

Lady Galwood nodded approvingly.

"I would like to invite you, Lady Galwood, and Lady Serafine, to a dinner at my home, tomorrow evening, in celebration of our most successful business venture. Will you do me the honour of attending?"

Lady Galwood inclined her head regally, and smiled, drawing Sera to her side.

"We shall be delighted Mr Morton."

"Excellent – I will send Alf to collect you at seven."

He took Sera's hand, and bent to kiss it, his lips lingering longer than usual, as he breathed in the unique scent of her, clean and fresh and touched with something faintly exotic.

"Until then."

"Thank you – for everything, Mr Morton." Sera's voice was soft, thready with exhaustion, rich with sincerity. He wondered if that 'everything' included the kiss.

Chapter Eleven

Sera stood in the foyer with her mother, awaiting Alf's arrival. She smoothed the soft wool fabric of her dress, and settled the silk shawl around her shoulders, her fur pelisse close to hand for when they must step out the door. New clothes, which she might once have barely regarded, were now a thing to treasure and appreciate – a year of poverty had taught her that. The wealth that had come with her business venture had given them back comfort, and dignity – she would never let herself forget the lessons of the last year.

It felt most odd to dress as a Lady for a dinner party, after so long. She wondered what Raphae's family would be like, and if her dress was appropriate. Her mother, it seemed, had no such doubts or questions, she simply stood, elegant as always, and waited, watching her daughter fidget with a fond smile.

There was a tap at the door, and Alf was there, ushering them to the carriage cheerfully, surrounded by a faint but pleasant scent of hay and warm horses.

It was not far, yet she was most glad of the carriage, for the chill of late winter was still sharp as the day closed in. Her fingers closed around the strings of her reticule, reassuring herself that its contents were still secure. Perhaps she was a fool, but perhaps this was the right decision. She would see.

~~~~~

They drew up outside a most impressive residence, considerably larger than their respectable but unfashionable dwelling. The sheer size of it made her nervous, but she pushed that aside. The doors opened onto a marble tiled hall, and a respectful footman took their outer garments. Another ushered them into a parlour.

It was a beautiful room, part panelled in rich inlaid timbers, part papered with a delicate Chinoiserie pattern of birds and bamboo, all in delicate gold tones, with tiny highlights of red. The chaises were covered in gold toned brocades, and a magnificent painting hung above the mantle. It resembled paintings by the Flemish masters, with late afternoon light on golden hills and fields, all under a sky of dramatic storm clouds with just a trace of blue. It was, she suspected, worth a fortune.

The door opened behind her, and she spun, somewhat embarrassed to have been caught gawking at her surroundings like someone who had never seen an elegant room before. Raphael was followed into the room by his mother, sister and brother, but, at first, she did not even see them. He looked as she had never seen him before.
~~~~~

In evening wear of the highest quality, of a cut that was both elegant, and yet displayed his form to perfection, he looked more the gentleman than any man of the *ton* she had ever met. Her lips parted in a little gasp of admiration, and her eyes locked with his, their dark depths drawing her in, the warmth of his gaze unmistakable. He hesitated a moment, then, blinking, looked away.

The rest of the room, and the people with him, came rushing back into focus. His mother was most definitely Italian, and age had in no way diminished her beauty. Sera could see immediately that Raphael's face echoed the elegant lines of hers.

"Mother, may I present the Dowager Lady Galwood, and her daughter, Lady Serafine Parkington."

Sera chose to honour Mrs Morton with a curtsey, although their respective ranks did not demand it. Raphael's eyes glowed with appreciation at her gesture.

"And Lady Galwood, Lady Serafine, may I present my mother, Mrs Sophia Morton, my sister, Miss Isabella Morton, and my brother, Mr Gabriel Morton."

Isabella performed a curtsey to match Sera's, and Gabriel managed a creditable, if slightly wobbly, bow. Gabriel showed al the signs of equalling Raphael's handsomeness in a few years' time, and Isabella was already a beauty – had she been a daughter of the *ton*, she would have quite been the toast of this Season.

There was a moment of silence, into which Lady Galwood smoothly inserted a gracious thanks for their invitation.

Mrs Morton swept forward to capture Lady Galwood's hands, and spoke, the lilt of Italy still in her voice, even after all the years that she had spent in England.

"I am delighted to meet you at last. My son has been full of extravagant praise for your daughter, and I must add my gratitude to you both. For Raphael was quite blue-devilled at first, upon his return to us – feeling the loss of his father, and readjusting to civilian life – this business venture has completely cured him of that state. Now, come, pray be seated, let us be comfortable together."

Sera blinked in some surprise at her words. Extravagant praise? For her? It was a startling concept. She found herself liking this forthright woman – very much. Raphael had, on hearing his mother's words, actually blushed – something she had not thought it possible to see. Perhaps, after all, she had made the right decision – her fingers unconsciously patted gently at her reticule, reassuring herself that its contents were safe.

They fell into comfortable conversation with ease, with Isabella excited to learn about how she had come to have the ideas for such beautiful designs, Gabriel asking slightly wistful questions about how young men of the *ton* spent their time and Mrs Morton setting them completely at ease, with witty and intelligent discussion on an astonishingly wide range of topics, including some rather tart, but accurate commentary on members of the *ton*.

It was a great insight for Sera, into how the merchant class saw the nobility, and on just how much they knew about the lives of the upper ten thousand, just from the goods sold to them.

It was, in fact, rather humbling. The courtesy and good cheer in this house quite outshone that of those of the Quality who had been her supposed friends... *before*... As dinner was announced, and they rose to proceed to the dining room, Sera came to a realisation which left her shaken to the core.

These people knew so much of the life and the gossip of the *ton*, it was impossible that Mrs Morton, at least, was unaware of their family scandal. Yet she had received them with sincere pleasure and grace, and seemed truly happy in their company. The kindness of soul demonstrated here nearly brought her to tears on the instant. For surely, if Italian, it was quite possible that Mrs Morton was of the papist church – who held taking one's own life as an even greater sin than did most. That she could look past that terrible blemish upon their family, and receive them with genuine warmth was a great gift.

As the dinner proceeded, Sera found herself relaxed and enjoying herself, engaged in discussions that ranged from the business plans for the next year to the comparative virtues of different fabrics, or the qualities required in a superior cologne or perfume, to Isabella's wistful desire to attend society Balls, even knowing that she would be looked down on. Although, as had often been commented in Society drawing rooms, *sotto voce*, a merchant's daughter with a very large dowry to accompany her beauty might often be forgiven her birth and seen as a suitable bride for a Lord in need of funds.

Raphael relaxed as the evening went on – he had, at least a little, been concerned that his family might not take to Sera – which would have made him most unhappy – although he did not inspect his reasons for that too closely.

The last course was removed, and the ladies retired to the parlour. As an acknowledgement of his growing maturity, Raphael retired to the library with Gabriel, and provided him with a glass of port. The boy's eyes lit up at being treated as an adult, and they sat for a while, talking of horses and vehicles, of boxing and fencing and other 'gentlemanly' topics, and only a little of business.

Eventually, though, the port had its effect, and Gabriel's eyes drooped. Raphael smiled at him, glad to see his brother happy.

"Off to bed with you, Gabriel, before you fall asleep in the chair."

Gabriel started, then placed his near empty glass on the side table with exaggerated care, nodded, and rose.

"I like her, Raphael, and I rather think that you like her more than you say, too. That's good, you should have someone to care about that way. Good night to you." Yawning, he left the room.

Raphael stood, open-mouthed in surprise for a moment, before turning and pouring himself a brandy that he felt a sudden need of.

It was very late, and the enjoyable evening would end soon. If she was going to do this, now was the time.

Sera rose and asked for the direction of the necessary, then quietly exited the room. But she did not follow the directions given. Instead, she made her way down the hall to the slightly ajar door of the room that she had seen Raphael enter, when they left the dining room.

Her heart beat hard, thumping almost painfully in her chest, and her palms felt damp with nerves. But she was determined. He might reject her gesture – if so, at least she would know where she stood. But he might not, and in that case, the future might hold things she had once though lost to her forever. At least there would be a chance.

She pushed the door open gently, stepped in, and just as gently pushed it closed behind her. The soft click of the closing door brought him round, from where he stood staring into the flames of the fire, to gaze instead, at her.

The soft amber colour of her gown made her golden eyes glow more brightly than usual, and the deep red highlights in her hair shone in the lamplight. He waited, bemused, as she walked to him and stopped.

"Raphael..." her voice had the same soft huskiness he had heard in the stable, but this time it was some emotion, not smoke, that had roughened her voice. He shivered at the sound, feeling it deep within him, in the place that had ached for her, all these sennights.

"I... I wanted to give you something." Her voice shook a little, but her smile was breathtaking. She lifted her reticule and undid its strings. Raphael watched, intrigued, waiting. Sera opened the reticule to its fullest extent, reached in, and very carefully withdrew something.

"Your hand, if you please."

Still bemused, he complied, holding out an open palm.

Delicately, as if handling a tiny bird, or something equally fragile, she laid something on his hand.

He dragged his eyes away from her face, and looked. On his hand lay a tiny favour, a heart made from beautiful antique lace, adorned with tiny beads of crystal and ruby, all stiffened by a piece of old, old vellum of the highest quality. If he had thought the favours she made for their business exquisite, then this was a step above and beyond them again.

He raised his eyes to hers, and she smiled, shyly, with uncertainty, but with something in her eyes that he had dreamed of, and barely hoped could ever be real.

"I made this some years ago... *before*... I put all of my wishes and longings into it, all of my memories of my grandmother, and the good things in my life, into this, made with her lace. It was a promise to myself, through all of the bad things. The heart of me. Now, I want to give it to you. It is near midnight. In but a few minutes, it will be Saint Valentine's Day. Please, accept my Valentine."

She stopped, and simply stood, watching his face. She was afraid, shaking, terrified that he would reject this, more vulnerable than she had ever felt in her life, and by her own actions. But she would not presume – she would wait upon his response.

Raphael lifted the tiny thing and studied it. It was imbued with the scent that he had come to know as hers, it was, in its way, as utterly beautiful as she, as much from its simplicity as from its complexity. He brought it to his lips and kissed it gently. Then he slid it carefully into the pocket inside his jacket, close against his heart. Perhaps his dreams had a chance, after all.

"Thank you. This is a gift beyond price. I will treasure it, as I treasure you, always."

He held out his hand again, and this time she placed her own in his. He drew her to him, enfolcing her in his arms as he had in the stable, and tilted his face against her hair, the silky softness and the scent of her arousing him, as no other woman had. After a moment, he raised his hand, and tilted her head up. Her eyes sparkled with unshed tears, and something more. Her lips were soft and inviting, reddened where she had nibbled at them in her nervousness.

He bent his head and kissed her, gently at first, his lips exploring the shape of hers, his tongue caressing, and then, after a moment, she responded, her lips opening to him, her body pressing to his, her hands coming up to encircle his neck, to tangle in his hair. The kiss deepened, and everything faded away, but the feel of her in his arms, and the taste of her on his lips.

As the clock gently chimed midnight, and it became Saint Valentine's Day, towards which they had both worked so hard, they explored each other in a kiss that went on, and on, and on. Neither wished to stop, for stopping might require words again. For now, the possibilities for their future, which were contained in touch, taste and scent, were all that they wanted, perhaps all that they would ever need.

The End.

Read more of Raphael and Serafine's story in 'Winning the Merchant Earl' coming in late 2017.

87

About the Author

Arietta Richmond has been a compulsive reader and writer all her life. Whilst her reading has covered an enormous range of topics, history has always fascinated her, and historical novels been amongst her favourite reading.

She has written a wide range of work, from business articles and other non-fiction works (published under a pen name) but fiction has always been a major part of her life. Now, her Regency Historical Romance books are finally being released. The Derbyshire Set is comprised of 10 novels (7 released so far). The 'His Majesty's Hounds' series is comprised of 11 novels, with the fourth having just been released.

She also has a standalone longer novel shortly to be released, and two other series of novels in development.

She lives in Australia, and when not reading or writing, likes to travel, and to see in person the places where history happened.

Be the first to know about it when Arietta's next book is released!

Sign up to Arietta's newsletter at

http://www.ariettarichmond.com

When you do, you will receive a free copy of the <u>subscriber exclusive</u> novella **'A Gift of Love',** a prequel to the Derbyshire Set series, which ends on the day that 'The Earl's Unexpected Bride' begins

This story is not for sale anywhere – it is absolutely exclusive to newsletter subscribers!

Books in the 'His Majesty's Hounds' Series

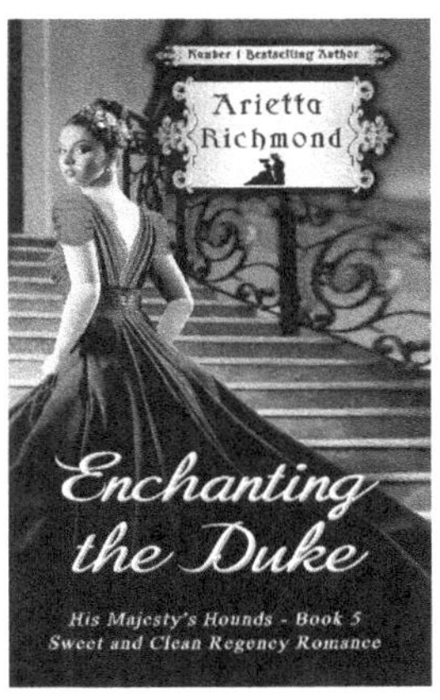

Redeeming the Marquess (coming soon)

Healing Lord Barton (coming soon)

Winning the Merchant Earl (coming soon)

Loving the Bitter Baron (coming soon)

Rescuing the Countess (coming soon)

Attracting the Spymaster (coming soon)

Here is your preview of

Claiming the Heart of a Duke

His Majesty's Hounds – Book 1
Sweet and Clean Regency Romance

Arietta Richmond

Chapter One

Having broken his fast at the inn that morning, Hunter Barrington, tenth Duke of Melton, had decided that he would ride for the last leg of his journey, because he was heartily sick of the stuffy carriage and of his valet's mournful mien.

This worthy, whom he had hired following his friend Raphael's advice (for it seemed that his business was a source of excellent information, not just imported goods), had vainly tried to turn him into a dandy during their short stay in London. Hunter smiled thinking of Bulwick's dismay when he had flatly refused to use the cane that Bulwick had tried to foist upon him, or to buy the inordinate number of fobs, which it was fashionable to attach to one's watch chain. After years in the field, his taste in dress was so simple that it could be called austere. Not so long ago, a day with clean clothes had been worth savouring, so all of this fuss seemed rather ridiculous to him.

Poor Bulwick had been horrified when he had declared his intention to ride.

"You can't possibly do that, my Lord," he had whispered.

"You will reach Meltonbrook Chase in a dishevelled and mussed condition. You will get a head cold, of a certainty. And, my Lord, if I may presume to comment further, the road is in very bad condition and frozen all over."

"Fustian!"

Hunter had exclaimed, shrugging away his valet's concern.

"It will do me good. Look after my luggage, Felton. I'm off."

The road, in his opinion, was quite good – certainly a vast improvement on trampled battlefields and roads in a war zone!

So, without further ado, he had swung onto his horse, leaving the bewildered valet with his mouth still open in protest.

For the first few miles, the ride had been exhilarating. Warmly clad in his greatcoat, beaver hat and fur lined gloves, astride his dapple grey stallion, he had delighted in the cold wind and in the speed-blurred landscape, as he let the stallion run off his energy.

The feeling of freedom, however, did not last long and had already vanished when Meltonbrook Chase appeared in the distance. It was the first time he had seen his family estate since his father, the late Duke, had purchased a commission for him, as was traditional for a second son.

Hunter could remember, perfectly well, his father's stern admonitions, imparted before sending him on his way to London, and hence to the Peninsular and war.

"Honour first of all, my son. Honour means more than life to our family. Never tarnish it, never demean yourself, never show a streak of the yellow. Remember, an officer and a nobleman must be an example for his men. England must stand against the French tyrant. Your commitment must be wholehearted. Your days as a dissipated and wild young buck have ended. Do you understand?"

'I thought I understood, Father, but I didn't. Only later, I did. Oh, yes, later I understood, all too well, what you meant.' Hunter's thought was wry, and a little sad.

He was so absorbed in his musings that he was barely registering the landscape. It took some time for him to realise that he was inside Meltonbrook Chase's expansive park. He reined in his horse, and stopped to look at the wintry landscape around him.

The silence was profound, broken only by the cawing of a crow, somewhere in the woods, and by the soft murmuring of the nearby brook.

The grounds were immaculate under the heavy pall of snow, the ice-traced tall poplars, which surrounded the lake, shining like silver filigree under the setting sun's slanting rays.

"I'm home." he thought, steeling himself for his first meeting with his family, after so many years.

Riding into the deserted stable yard, it seemed surreal that he was actually here – and even more surreal that his father and brother were gone, that all of this was his now.

He dismounted, the icy gravel crunching under his feet, as a brawny groom, in a leather coat, came running toward him.

"Master Hunter! Master Hunter! Is it you? Is it really you? At long last you're home again!" The man suddenly checked and lowered his head.

"Begging your pardon, Your Grace. I've been overfamiliar, but me happiness made me tongue run away with me, it did, old fool that I am."

"Never you mind, Nick. Master Hunter it is, if you wish it, as long as you keep it just between us. You know how stuffy my mother can be... Now, this is Nuage...." he gestured to the horse, which snuffled curiously at the old groom. "I bought him in France, and a valiant fellow he is. Take good care of him, will you? Go with Nick, my boy, he's a good one."

Nick stroked the horse's silky coat and took the reins.

"Always been a good judge of horseflesh, Master Hunter. Since you was a stripling, you was. Come along Nuage, a good rubdown is what you need right now. And what about some clean straw to lie on and some oats to chew?" Talking to the horse, the head groom disappeared around the corner toward the stable, as the carriage, bearing his valet, and his meagre luggage, drew up before the house.

~~~~~~~~

Nerissa looked at her reflection in the tall mirror and sighed.

She would never be an Incomparable, and that was that. Her colouring was all wrong, she was too tall and her face was too angular. In the pale pastel colours that were deemed fashionable for young ladies, she faded into insignificance.
~~~~~~~~

She sighed again, thinking of her sister Maria, an acknowledged Beauty, who had cut a triumphant swathe through the *ton* during the previous Season. It had been fashionable to be in love with Maria, with her flashing amber eyes, rich auburn hair and flawless creamy complexion.

Thus, Maria had had the opportunity of choosing from amongst a veritable army of suitors and was now betrothed - very advantageously betrothed, to be sure, to a wealthy Earl, to their parents' delight.

Donning her fur lined pelisse and her velvet bonnet, Nerissa crossed the hall and stepped into the carriage with her maid, bound to Meltonbrook Chase, where she was to have tea with her bosom bow Alyse, the Duke of Melton's daughter.

No, not daughter, sister, she amended her thought. Hunter was Duke, now, after the untimely demise of his father and his elder brother.

She blushed. They hoped that Hunter would be home soon, for he had sent his family a message from London, but with the deep snow on the roads, he was likely delayed.

Would he recognise her? She did not think so. He had had scant interest to spare for her, to begin with, when he was a young man just back from his term in Oxford, and she was just a shy ten year old, all angles and elbows and not even a promise of feminine allure.

Nerissa leaned back on the carriage seat, closing her eyes. *'Much good it does me to wool-gather like that'*, she chided herself. *'I'll be lucky if I don't find myself married to some gouty old man before the Season is over.'*

She shivered, and not because of the sharp wind blowing and howling through the naked trees.

~~~~~~~~

As Hunter approached the door, the butler, a delighted expression lighting his usually impassive features, opened it. Immediately regaining his formal demeanour, Jermyn schooled his expression to a more serious face, better suited to the Butler of a great house.

"Welcome home, my lord. The ladies are in the drawing room. Follow me, please."

"No need, Jermyn, I know the way", answered Hunter, secretly amused by the butler's display of self-restraint, and almost ran to the drawing room doors, suddenly unable to wait any longer to see his family.

He opened the doors, and an instant of shocked silence followed his entrance.

Hunter scanned the tableau – a morning visit frozen before him. All of his family were there (although part of his mind still expected to see his father and Richard as well), and there was someone else.

A woman he did not know, a woman who was more beautiful than any he had seen.

She had burnished golden hair, surrounding her face with a profusion of waves and ringlets, a honey and gold complexion; long, almond shaped green gold eyes, fringed by thick burnished golden eyelashes and emphasized by high cheekbones, and a tall, shapely body.
~~~~~~~~

The only feature detracting from perfection, but greatly adding to character, was a rather large, mobile mouth, much more capable of expressing feelings (and temper, he suspected!) than a proper prim little rosebud. He was captivated. Her eyes met his across the room, and for a moment, everything else faded away.

He was brought back to the moment when the silence was broken by his sister Alyse, who cried out: "Hunter! Hunter, you are back! Is it really you, Hunter?" and, without any further ado, threw herself at him. His eye contact with the woman was broken, and he forgot her in the chaos that followed.

Hunter's mother, the Duchess Louisa, half-fainting, reclined on the sofa, fanning herself and calling for her vinaigrette. His sister Sybilla, almost jigged around the table, before forcing herself to behave with greater propriety. His brother, Charles, obviously tried to be the cool gentleman, but could not help but step forward and embrace Hunter, his eyes shining with held back tears.

"At long last, my son," sobbed his mother.

"Come here, and let me look at you. Last time I saw you, you were a boy. Now you are a man. And what a man! Your father, God rest his soul, would be so proud of you…"

Moved despite himself, Hunter gathered his weeping mother into his arms.

"Shush, Mother, I'm here to stay. I'm so sorry I was not here when it would have really mattered. I feel that I have failed you all, yet it was at the time of Waterloo, and I did not even hear the news for months! I'm so sorry…"

The Duchess brushed her tears impatiently aside.

"I'm a foolish old woman, my son. This is not a time for weeping, but a time for rejoicing. God knows, we have been mourning long enough. And look who is here, Hunter. Do you remember Lady Nerissa Loughbridge, Lord Chester's youngest daughter?"

A faint recollection of a meddlesome brat, always trying to follow him around, vaguely stirred in Hunter's memory.

He turned his head and froze again, caught by her appearance.

Brat? She was not a brat anymore, she was a woman, and a very beautiful woman at that, more so because of her unusual colouring.

It was all he could do not to stare at her with his mouth agape. He tried to react in some polite way, and smiled, suddenly recalling one of Nerissa's youthful misdeeds.

"Nerissa? Was it you who hid inside your brother Kevin's portmanteau, because you wanted to come with us when we went to our hunting lodge near Cottesmore? And did we not discover you because you sneezed? Do you remember, Charles?"

Nerissa had not heard a single word.

Hunter's sudden appearance had completely stunned her.

All her childhood emotions flooded back, crowding her mind, amplified with new meaning and significance. A rosy blush washed upon her face as she dared to smile back.

"She's not a child anymore, Hunter," broke in Alyse.

"She is a dear friend to us all, and I really don't know how we would have managed without her. She is a sensible young woman, with a good head on her shoulders, and she gave us invaluable help when Mother was so ill after…" Alyse's voice faltered "…after the accident…"

Hunter looked at his family: his sisters, pretty, vivacious, eager to try out their wings during the London Season, his mother, with her gentle face marked by loss and sorrow, his brother, suddenly scowling and dark browed, and the enchanting stranger in their midst. He felt rather like he had stepped into the centre of a whirlwind.

Suddenly he felt mortally tired, in dire need of rest and solitude.

He went to his mother and kissed her gently on her cheek.

"Will you please excuse me, Mother? I have had a long and tiring journey and I'm much fatigued. I believe that, if you will forgive me, I will have a bath drawn and a tray sent to my room. I am not really up to a formal supper. Tomorrow, we can all begin to catch up."

"But of course, my dear. How thoughtless of me not having foreseen your needs… my happiness at seeing you again quite overwhelmed me. I have not all my wits about me, I'm sure… Jermyn, please, see His Grace to his apartments and make sure that his valet attends him."

"Yes, my lady. Please follow me, Your Grace."

To his chagrin, Jermyn did not lead Hunter to his bachelor's quarters as he had unthinkingly expected, but to his father's apartments.

That was the precise moment at which the full import of his new condition crashed in upon him like a dark and overwhelming wave.

He was the Duke of Melton.

Not his father, nor his elder brother, both now dead after a freak carriage accident. Himself.

He had not wanted it, he had not coveted it, truth to tell, he had no idea how to go about being a Duke, but there it was, with all its implications and obligations, including the need to marry, and to sire heirs to the title.

It was like a bad dream, but it was not going to disappear at dawn.

Regency Collections in Collaboration with Other Authors

Books in 'The Derbyshire Set'

Available at all good book stores and for ebook readers too!

Coming Soon!

Other Books from Dreamstone Publishing

Dreamstone publishes books in a wide variety of categories – here are some of our other bestselling books:-

We have books in many categories, ranging from Erotica and Romance to Kids Books, Books on Writing, Business Books, Photography, Cook Books, Diaries, Coloring books and much more. New books are released each month.

Be the first to know when our next books are coming out

Be first to get all the news – sign up for our newsletter at

http://www.dreamstonepublishing.com